FLIGHT
OF THE
FIRE
THIEF

KINGFISHER
a Houghton Mifflin Company imprint
222 Berkeley Street
Boston, Massachusetts 02116
www.houghtonmifflinbooks.com

First published in 2006
2 4 6 8 10 9 7 5 3 1

LIBRARY OF CONGRESS CATALOGING-IN-PUBLICATION DATA
has been applied for.

ISBN-13: 978-0-7534-5819-8
ISBN-10: 0-7534-5819-5

Printed in India
1TR/0506/TCL/MAR/50CM/C

FLIGHT
OF THE
FIRE
THIEF

TERRY DEARY

KINGFISHER
BOSTON

ONE

GREECE—AROUND 4,000 YEARS AGO

I wasn't there myself, but I met someone who knows exactly what went on in those days. You will have to trust me when I tell you that every word of this story is true . . . probably. All right, a LOT of it is true. Other parts I may have made up to fill in the gaps so that it all makes sense. Yes, you'll see that I tell a lot of lies. But liars are the only people you CAN trust in this world.

Zeus sat on a cloud.

You can do that sort of thing when you're a Greek god. But YOU shouldn't try it. You would need a very long ladder to get up to the clouds, and as soon as you stepped off, you would probably fall clean through the cloud. This could get very messy—

especially if someone is walking underneath you.

Only special people like me and my pa could sail up and over the clouds. How could I do that? Wait and see.

Where was I? Oh, yes, Zeus on his cloud. He wore wings and was the most beautiful thing you've ever seen—so beautiful that ordinary people (like you and me) couldn't bear to look at him.[1]

Next to Zeus sat his wife, Hera, and she was not so beautiful because she had a scowl on her face. Her nose crinkled like a caterpillar's back, and her lips were as thin as an ant's leg.

"You promised me a vacation," she snapped.

"This is a vacation, dearest," Zeus said and smiled. "A sparkling blue sea and miles of sandy beach."

"The beach is covered with human corpses!" she screeched.

"There's a war on, my lovely," her husband said with a shrug. "We can sit and watch it just as those humans watch their little plays at the theater."

Hera pouted. "I wouldn't know. You never take me

---

1   "Aha!" you cry. "Last week I was starving, and a cheese sandwich was the most beautiful thing I'd ever seen! More beautiful than a Greek god." All I can say is this: if you keep crying out like that, I'll never get on with my story. So stop arguing and listen.

to the theater."

"This is real life—much more fun," he argued. "We can even join in."

"You are too mean to take me to the theater. You're so mean that you'd steal a dead fly from a blind spider."

"Only if you were feeling hungry," he muttered.

Hera didn't hear. Just as well.

"The town stinks," she said. "Humans stink. I don't know why you don't just send down a thunderbolt and burn it to the ground. A good fire would clean it up."

"Ah, fire," Zeus said and nodded. "They don't need my fire. The humans can make fire for themselves."

Hera turned to him with a face as sharp as a shrew. "And who *gave* them the power of fire?"

"I know," Zeus said and sighed.

Hera slapped and plumped up the cloud to make herself more comfortable. "I asked you a question, Zeus. Who gave them fire?"

"My cousin Prometheus," Zeus said and closed his eyes. He was wishing that he hadn't mentioned it.

"Yes, your cousin Theus! He stole fire from the gods and gave it to those creeping little, fighting little, *stinking* little humans."

"Don't get on my back. I have punished him . . ." Zeus began.

"Oh, you *punished* him. You had him chained to a rock. And every day the Avenger came down in the shape of an eagle and ripped out his liver. What sort of punishment is that?" Hera snapped, and thundery sparks crackled in the cloud.

"Every night the liver grew back, so he had to suffer the agony every day for two hundred years . . ." Zeus argued and grew angry as the cloud grew dark.

"But what happened? Eh? What happened?" Hera sneered. "You let him escape!"

"I didn't exactly *let* him . . ."

"All right. You let Hercules *rescue* him. Same difference. And where is Theus now? Hiding. He's traveled through time and space, and he could be anywhere. The poor little Avenger has worn out its wings looking for him!"

"*Poor? Little?* It's a blooming great bird with the sharpest beak this side of Mount Olympus. Its talons can rip a rhino's skin . . ."

"Don't argue with me, Zeus. You always lose," Hera said with a shake of her head. "Theus gave fire to the humans, and he got away with it. I only hope that the

8

Avenger finds him one day. It's still out there searching!"

Zeus propped himself up on an elbow. "I *did* make Theus a promise, my dear. I gave him a challenge. I said that if he could find one true human hero, I'd forgive him!"

Hera snorted . . . and then her nose twitched as the stench from the city slipped into her nostrils. "He'll fail. He'll never find a human hero. The Avenger will find Theus first."

"The Avenger will be a bit busy, my dear," Zeus said and peered over the edge of the cloud to the city by the sea below. "There will be a lot of warriors here who need to be taken down to Hades and the underworld. I'm tired of this Troy."

"You're like a baby," Hera said and laughed bitterly. "You soon get tired of a new toy."

"I said *Troy*, not *toy*," Zeus said with a sniff. "The Greeks have been trying to take the city for *ten years* now—*that's* not getting tired *quickly*! Ten *years*!"

Hera rolled over and lay on her stomach next to her husband. The gods gazed down.

Inside the city the ragged Trojans trudged through the streets, thin and weary from the endless war. With secret tunnels and hidden doors, enough food had slipped into the city to keep them going for ten years. Bottomless wells of sweet water would last them forever. But the spirit of the people was as threadbare as their clothes. They longed for freedom. Freedom from a city that had become a prison— freedom from the fear that their prison walls would fall and let in sharp, slicing, stabbing death.

There were no rats in the city of Troy. They'd all been eaten long ago.

Outside the city a thousand Greek ships rested and rotted on the hot shore. Tattered tents stood, faded and patched, flapping in the warm wind that blew over the soft sand. Slouching soldiers sat on rocks, polished their worn weapons for the $3,600^{th}$ time, and longed for home.

"So, what are you going to do about it, husband?" Hera asked.

"Put an end to it," Zeus said.

Hera nodded. "And would you like me to tell you who is going to win?"

Zeus's shoulders dropped. "You are going to anyway."

Hera gave a small smile like a cat that's cornered a bowl of milk. "The Greeks are going to enter Troy. They are going to kill the pathetic Prince Paris and his hideous Helen."

"I thought you might say that," Zeus muttered. Hera held a big grudge against Paris and Helen. Ten years ago the goddesses held a beauty contest, and Prince Paris was the judge. Hera offered the judge power over all of Asia. Athena, the goddess of war, offered him victory wherever he fought. Aphrodite, the goddess of love, offered him the gift of the most beautiful woman in the world. And everyone knew that was Helen of Sparta.

Paris chose Aphrodite as the winner and won the hand of Helen. Hera chose to sulk.

"I hate Helen! Hate her, *hate her*, *HATE HER!*" she cried.

"You don't like her then?" Zeus said with a smile.

"I can't TELL you how much I hate her," she screamed, and the cloud shivered and shook out a storm of raindrops onto the dusty heads of the Trojans below. "She is *not* the most beautiful woman in the world—her hair is too straight, her nose is too short, and as for her ears . . . well, what can I say about a woman with ears like that?"

"And she's married to Menelaus, of course," Zeus added, stoking up his wife's rage.

"Ooooh! Yes! A faithless woman. Married to poor

King Menelaus, and still she ran off with Paris of Troy."
Hera pulled back her lips in a savage sneer. "Her Troy
boy!" she said and looked pleased with her little joke.
"And just look at the trouble she's caused," she added
with a sweep of her hand at the scene below. "A
thousand ships and fifty thousand soldiers sent to take
her back to Greece. Me? I'd leave her to rot in Troy.
From the smell of the place, it is rotting already."

Zeus sniffed and nodded.

Hera turned quickly to Zeus. "So? Whose side are
you going to join? If you let *Troy* win, then I will
make you wish that you lived in Hades with all of
the tortures that the humans suffer there after death."

Zeus held up his mighty hands. "Oh, don't worry,
wife. Troy will *lose* because the old curse says that
Paris will bring about the destruction of the city.
We can't go against the old curses," Zeus said.

"The old curse also says that the Greek hero
Achilles will die in Troy." She jabbed a finger at the
Greek tents on the plains of Troy. "He's still alive."[2]

2 Hera and Zeus could SEE Achilles wandering around the camp
because they had incredible eyesight. If you could fly, like me, you would
see people on the ground like ants. But the gods had eyes like telescopes
(binoculars?). Amazing but true.

Zeus rubbed his eyes tiredly. "Yes, there's so much to do. I don't know where to start."

"Send for the Avenger," Hera told him. "It'll be handy to have it around when Achilles and Paris are killed. The Avenger can take them straight to Hades."

Zeus nodded, placed his fingers on his lips, and gave a whistle that shook the walls of Troy. It also made Hera's ears ring.

"Must you?"

"I have to send for Hermes, our messenger."

"Right. *Then* you need to arrange for Achilles to die . . . and *then* you have to make sure that the Greeks get inside Troy and kill Paris."

Zeus nodded slowly. "Yes, that's what I need to do," he agreed.

Hera puffed out her cheeks and blew with pride— which caused a sandstorm on the beach and tattered the tents again. "Phooey! I honestly don't know *what* you'd do without me, Zeus," she said.

"I'd like a chance to find out," he muttered under his breath.

"What was that?"

"I said, dear, I think you've blown some fires out!"

"Fires out? What are you talking about, Zeus?"

"Nothing, dear," the great god said and then turned as he heard a fluttering of wings. A young man landed on the cloud, wearing a bag at his waist. He held a wooden rod with snakes twined around it. There were wings on his sandals and wings on his helmet and a spoiled look on his face. "Ah, here's Hermes," Zeus said.

"What do you want this time, my foul stepfather?" Hermes said with a sigh.

Zeus took a deep breath and held his temper. It wasn't easy.

"I want you to find the Avenger and bring it to Troy."

Hermes threw down his rod, and the shocked snakes hissed in their surprise. "Ooh! He wants me to find the Avenger. Just like that? I say, just like that?"

Zeus punched the cloud in anger ... but punching clouds doesn't do you much good. He began to speak quickly in a low, angry voice. "Hermes, you are the messenger of the gods, and it is your job to take messages. So will you please stop complaining about it and get on with what you are paid to do?"

Hermes blinked. "Paid? When have you ever *paid*

14

me? I am rushed off my winged feet, morning to night and night to morning. And not *only* do I not get paid, but I don't even get any *thanks*. All I get is shouted at!" He pulled at the hem of his tunic and blew his nose on it.

"You've made Hermes cry now," Hera groaned. "Say you're sorry, Zeus."

"You're sorry, Zeus," the god growled and then turned back to the sniffling messenger. "Hermes. *Please* do this small thing for me, and I will be so very grateful that I will never shout at you again."

"Promise?" Hermes said and sniffed.

"Promise," Zeus said. "The Avenger is traveling through time looking for Cousin Theus. Theus and the Avenger were last seen in a place called Eden City in a time the humans call 1858."

"Time? I have to travel through time?" Hermes screeched.

"We'll be *so-o* very grateful," Hera told him. "We'll have a special party for you when you get back."

Hermes' face lit up. "A party? With cupcakes?"

"Yes, dear," Hera said. She picked up the hissing rod and handed it to him. "Now, off you go, through time. Tell the Avenger that we're in Troy."

As Hermes' wings began to beat like a hummingbird, Zeus waved. "Have a nice *time!*"

Hera rubbed her hands together. "That's that problem solved. Now . . . *how* are you going to kill Achilles?" she asked.

Zeus smirked. "I have a rather neat little plan, my dear. A brilliant plan, a work of a genius, even if I do say so myself."

"Hmm!" Hera said. "We'll see."

★★★

Somewhere, just beyond the farthest star, the Greek demigod Prometheus drifted on white wings.

It was lonely out there. He headed for home.

TWO

EAST RIVER CITY—1795

This time I really WAS there. This is my story, so I know it happened. I was just a 12-year-old girl at the time, but I remember it as clearly as if it was the day before yesterday . . . even though it was more than 60 years ago. I may be getting old, but there are some things you NEVER forget. And being shot by my own pa is one of them . . .

I used to hate it when Pa shot me. Sometimes he did it twice a day, and that made me hurt all over.

That windy afternoon in East River City was no different. I'd been up since daybreak helping fill the balloon with hot air. By afternoon it was higher than a ten-story building and straining at the ropes that held it to the ground in the city park.

Pa had painted the white paper balloon with red stripes, and big black letters told the world, "Dr. Dee and his amazing Carnival of Danger!"

The people of East River City couldn't miss it, and they were starting to gather in the park. Kids with runny noses formed lines to buy my apples dipped in caramel or my sugar canes, my popcorn, and my sugared almonds. "We should charge people to see the show," I grumbled one day.[3]

"No need, Nellie," he said and laughed. "If people have to pay to come, they'll stay away. Tell them they're getting something for *nothing,* and they'll flock along. That makes it easier to take their money when they get here! People are suckers like that," he said and tapped the side of his nose. He did that to show that he was the wisest man in the world. He wasn't.

So we made our money by selling cheap food at five times what it was worth and passing a hat around the crowd after each amazing danger. The

3 I did a lot of grumbling. This is NOT because I am a moaner. It's because Pa gave me a lot to grumble about. If your pa shot you twice a day, then YOU would grumble and whine a lot more than I do. You look like a grumbler and a whiner to me, so don't you go complaining if I moan from time to time!

people paid up. I remember that afternoon and the kid in the sailor suit. "Hey!" he squawked. "I bit into this apple and found a worm!"

"Wow!" I gasped. "You lucky, lucky boy! That's a rare apple you have there."

"It is?"

"Why, yes. Only one apple in a hundred has a magic worm inside it. We usually charge *double* for apples with a magic worm inside."

"Magic? What does it do?" the kid asked.

"Do? Why . . . it . . . it . . . has the power to make you invisible," I told him.

He looked down at his sailor suit. "I can still see me," he argued.

"Ah, you have to wait till midnight and then ask the worm nicely." I knew that by midnight we'd be miles away, and he'd never get his money back. Pa's rule was never give the suckers their money back.

The kid looked at the apple. "But I bit it in half," he said and frowned.

"Ah! Shame! Then you'll never get to be invisible." I sighed. "You really should have been more careful," I scolded. "Now, are you going to pay me double for that special apple, or do I have to tell your ma and pa that you tried to sneak off with a magic apple without paying?"

The kid turned pale. "N–no!"

I held out my hand. His trembling little paw pressed a coin into mine. He backed away, as scared as a rabbit in a dog's dinner bowl.

Feel sorry for the kid, do you? Pa told me never to feel sorry for the suckers. But I guess I have a soft inside compared to my tough outside. I would *never* tell Pa this, but that afternoon I felt a touch of real pity for the poor little worm that got eaten in half.

It's a tough life.

"Time to close the stall and get ready for the show, Nellie," Pa said.

"Don't call me Nellie," I muttered.

"It's your name," he lied.

You see, my name is Helen. Some clever person decided it would be funny to turn the name backward, and girls named Helen often get called Neleh . . . or Nellie. Now I didn't mind Helen and I could live with Nell, but I never liked Nellie. So, if it's all right with you, I'll call myself Nell in this story so that you don't get confused with the other Helen . . . the one with a face so beautiful that they launched a thousand ships to find her.[4]

"Call me Nell, Pa," I said. "Or I won't do the show."

He knew I meant it. Pa and I got along well because we'd learned how to handle one another. Pa may tell the world that he had the most amazing Carnival of Danger, but we both knew that I was the one who did the dangerous parts. He was just the showman who sold them.

I swept up the cloth with the candy and dropped it into the basket of the balloon. I checked that the fire below the balloon was smoking nicely and ducked down to change into my first costume. It was a baggy silk suit with blue-and-yellow stripes, a black mustache, and black boots.

I needed those boots to save my soles. Being shot by your pa can hurt your heels and slap your soles till you're sore.

By the time I was ready, Pa was standing on a box and calling to the crowd.

"Welcome to Dr. Dee's most amazing Carnival

4 Yes, dear reader, even though we were born 4,000 years apart, Helen of Troy and I would end up in the same tale. Of course, I was more beautiful than Helen of Troy—I mean, when you get to be 4,000 years old, you must have a few wrinkles.

of Danger!" he roared. He had a good voice, did Pa. "This afternoon you will see my talented team of plucky performers daring to defy death."

He had the crowd gripped now. They'd fallen silent, and he was able to lower his voice. "In fact, my friends, I have to warn you that some of them may *not* survive the dangers. Some days, Death wins. If you are upset by the sight of mangled bodies and bleeding corpses, then please go home now . . ."

Of course, no one moved. The suckers went to our shows *hoping* to see some disasters. Our goal was to disappoint them. At least that was *my* goal. You see, there was no talented "team" of plucky performers. There was just me. Little Nellie Dee. I did all the stunts. Dr. Dee's amazing Carnival of Danger was me and Pa. I just changed costumes and wigs under the cover of the balloon basket while Pa kept the crowd's attention with the big buildups.

"And for our first death-defying display we have . . . all the way from Russia . . ." (pause while the crowd goes, "Ooh!") ". . . the magnificent . . . the masterful . . . the miraculous . . . Gregory . . . the-e-e-e . . . Grrrreat!"

I stepped forward and bowed stiffly to the

cheering crowd but kept moving quickly so that they couldn't see the ribbons that held my mustache in place or the high heels on the boots that made me look taller.

I stood next to the wooden cannon and faced the dark muzzle. I gripped it, raised myself up, placed my feet inside the barrel, and let myself slide down. As I slid into the gloom, I twisted so that I was facedown. (I hated it when I shot out on my back and found myself looking up at the clouds.)

Pa's voice and the cheering of the crowd were muffled down there. I knew that he was going on about the danger of me breaking my neck if he fired the cannon and I missed the safety net. Pa was a great liar, but that part was true!

He always made out like it was a real cannon filled with gunpowder. In fact, it was a wooden cannon with a big spring. When he lit the fuse, he burned through a piece of cord that held back the spring. When the cord burned through, the spring sprang and threw me out. There was a flash and a pop, and I was flying.

Now Pa's a phony and a faker, but he's good at his job. He always made sure that I hit that net. As I grew older and heavier, he changed the power of the spring and never made any mistakes. I was too precious. After all, where would he find another cannonball if he killed me? Especially after what happened to Ma . . . but that's another story.

Yet that afternoon in East River City was cursed. It could have been the east wind that whipped over the sea, or it could have been that our luck had to run out some time.

Inside the barrel of the wooden cannon I heard the sizzle of the fuse and screwed up my face, waiting for the shock of the spring smacking into my feet.

Sizzle . . . twing[5] . . . whoosh . . . thunk!

I felt the sting on my feet. The barrel was smooth and waxed. My costume was silk, so rushing out didn't graze or burn me. Then the air filled my lungs with a great rush, as if someone was stuffing a pillow down my throat. My mustache slapped against my cheeks, and my eyes watered.

Then I reached the top of my curve and slowed. This was where I'd tuck up my knees, do a somersault

---

5 This is the sound of the cord snapping—it's a cross between a singing and a twanging. A twing, in fact. You may not have heard this word before. You have now.

to make the crowd gasp, and then spread my arms and legs, like a flying frog, to drop into the net . . . usually.

But that afternoon the wind was from my right side. Pa *never* allowed that to happen. The wicked wind must have switched direction. I felt myself being pushed to the left of the net. I twisted in the air and rolled to my right like a spinning bullet.

Even at that height, I heard the crowd gasp. *This* was what they'd come to see . . . a Russian cannonball a-rushin' to the ground. I thought I was a goner. Was this how the worm felt as the kid's teeth crunched into the apple?

I twisted again and used my legs to kick out and swim against the air. The edge of the net was almost out of reach as I hurtled toward it. I grabbed at it and got my right hand on the edge and held tight.

The force almost tore my arm out of my shoulder, and I had to let go. I dropped to the ground but had slowed myself enough to save my life. That's not to say that it didn't hurt. It did. I landed on my feet, and the blow almost rattled my teeth out of my head. My wig and mustache were twisted, and all I could think was to set them straight, take a bow, and rush back to the balloon to change.

My knees were weak—either from the shock or the fall—and I wobbled away to the balloon basket as the crowd cheered.

I flung off the blue-and-yellow costume and changed into a pink ballet dress to appear as Miss Cobweb from England. I climbed up onto the high wire and danced along the tightrope. The wind pushed me, and when I leaned toward it, the wind dropped and left me tottering. I always liked to put in a totter or two to excite the crowd, but that day it was for real.

As Captain Dare, in a tight black swimsuit and leather helmet, I dived from a high platform into a shallow pool of water. Just for fun, the water was covered in a film of burning oil that roared in the wind. A gust blew me hard toward the left, so I jumped to the right and hoped that it would blow me back toward the small circle of flaming water. As I threw myself off the board, the wind dropped a little and made me fall dangerously close to the right side. Somehow I hit the pool and pulled myself out. This time I dressed myself in dungarees, a cotton shirt, and a canvas jacket. Pa climbed in beside me.

"You did well, Nell," he muttered. He jangled a leather bag full of cash and stored it carefully in the bottom of the basket.

"We can't take the balloon up in this wind," I hissed.

"We can. Trust me—I'm a doctor," he said and shrugged.

"A what?"

"A doctor! Dr. Dee!" he explained.

"No, you're not! You just invented that name! You're not *really* a doctor of science or anything else!" I reminded him.

"Maybe not." He shrugged. "We'll be all right . . . we'll just take her up a little way," he promised. Then he began announcing our final "danger."

"My friends . . . you will now witness the first-ever flight by a human being in this country. Direct from Paris, this balloon was built by the Montgolfier brothers themselves . . ."

The wind was whining in the ropes that held the balloon to the basket. The ropes were tight as it strained to lift upward. The wind was making the straw-and-wool fire burn too hot.

"We can't take the balloon up!" I groaned at Pa.

He wasn't listening. He had already chosen four heavy men in the audience to pull us back down after we'd risen a hundred feet in the air.

"Prepare to watch and wonder!" he cried and pulled the slipknot that set us free.

The balloon rose like a rocket and threw us down into the basket. We soon reached the end of the rope that tied us to the ground. The speed was too fast. The rope snapped. The four men found that they were being lifted off the ground, so they dropped their ropes and set us free. One tried to tie his rope to our cannon, but, being made out of wood, it had no weight.

The crowd on the ground below was just a blur of gaping faces. We were in free flight for the first time ever.

"Oh, dear," Pa said and sighed. "Oh, dear, oh, dear, oh, *dear*!"

I looked over the side and saw the city slip away below us. "Great," I groaned. "Dr. D . . . 'D' for disaster."

THREE

TROY—AROUND 4,000 YEARS AGO

There are two stories going on here. At some time—I don't know when—they will join up to make one story. Now, I don't want you to forget what was going on back in Greece. So we'll leave me floating off to disaster in the balloon . . . don't worry about me—I'll survive somehow—and we'll go back to the plot to smash Troy.

Paris stood on the walls of his palace and pouted. "I wish those Greeks would go away," he said and sighed.

"You say that every day," Helen reminded him. Her face had been lovely enough to launch a thousand ships. But ten years of frowning had creased that face a bit. These days she'd have been be lucky to launch 900 ships.

"It's that Achilles," Paris said. "He's such a hero

that he'll *never* give up."

"You say *that* every day too," Helen said. "You could be getting a teeny bit boring, Paris dear. I ran away from Menelaus because *he* was so boring."

"And because he never washed his feet, you said. He was a smelly old man," Paris reminded her.

"And when was the last time that you washed *your* feet, Paris my petal?"

He sniffed. "Last week . . . I'm saving on soap. There's a war on, you know."

"I know . . . oh, I know," Helen muttered. "I'm just off to see my dressmaker," she said and glided along the platform behind the wall like an elegant lady. A lady so elegant that she could launch at least 800 ships with that windburned face.

"If only I could get rid of Achilles," Paris muttered.

"You *could*," a Trojan soldier said.

If Paris had been paying attention, then he'd have noticed that there was no Trojan soldier there a moment ago. A sprinkle of cloud dust had fallen behind him and taken the shape of a warrior.

Now YOU know that soldier was really Zeus who had shape-shifted—but Paris wasn't very bright, and he was too worried and wearied by war to notice.

"Could what, captain?" Paris asked.

"Oh, mighty Paris, sir, my lord, I be only a poor and 'umble sergeant. I be not one of your great and good cap'ns, your holiness!" Zeus said.[6]

"Did you know, sergeant, that Helen told me that my feet smell? What do you think of that?"

"With all respect, mighty Paris, I be thinking 'er ladyship, she be mistaking herself. Why, every Trojan vagrant and tickle monger[7] would tell you that feet don't smell. Lordy, no sir. It be noses that smell, sir! Not feet! Feet's for walking on, not for smelling. Why if your ole feet smelled, then every time you stepped in a pile of horse droppings in the street, you'd . . ."

"Thank you, sergeant. Can you tell me how to get rid of Achilles?"

"I'm glad you asked me that, sir. As it be

6   Yes, I know that this is a curious and ungodly way to talk. But there were two reasons for it. Firstly, Zeus was only guessing how a Trojan sergeant might talk. Secondly, Zeus enjoyed a bit of playacting, so he always went a bit over-the-top when he appeared to humans. Let's be honest—he was just a god-awful actor.

7   A Trojan tickle monger was a clown who sold tickles to his audience . . . in Troy. Sadly, they all died out in Roman times when tickling was made illegal by the emperor Vespasian, and tickle mongers were thrown to the crocodiles in the Colosseum.

happening, I be knowing a way to be doing away with the awful Achilles," Zeus said.

"By Zeus, you're a better man than me if you can do it!" Paris said and slapped the god on his back.

"There be a legend about that there Achilles, there be, sir . . ."

"I know it!" Paris said and sighed. "His mother was Thetis . . ."

"Nice lass," Zeus said with a nod.

"You knew her?"

"Well!"

"Anyway, Thetis was a goddess, and she wanted her son Achilles to be safe in battle. So, when he was a baby, she dipped him in the River Styx in the underworld. That way he couldn't be harmed. But . . ."

"Ah, *but* . . ." Zeus went on, "she held him by the heel . . ."

"And the heel was the only part that wasn't touched by the charmed waters," Paris finished.

"So?" Zeus said and nodded.

"So what?"

Zeus rolled his eyes. This Paris wasn't very bright. "*So-o-o* . . . if someone was going to attack him, then *where* would they attack him?"

Paris scratched his head under his long and flowing hair. "Er? In bed when he's asleep?"

"No . . . I mean where on his body would you strike him? You'd have to strike him on the heel—his weak spot."

Paris blinked. "*ME* strike him? Who says *I'm* going to strike him?"

Zeus sighed. "No one else is going to do it for you, my great and mighty lord."

"He's a wondrous warrior. I might get hurt!" Paris argued. "Did you not see what he did to our greatest fighter, Hector? First he killed him, had his corpse dragged around Troy, and then he fed him to the dogs! I don't want to end up as a doggy dinner, thank you very much!"

"You won't. Not if you use a sneaky plot, sir."

"Ah, I'll have to think of one."

"I have one, mighty lord."

"You have? Good man . . . er, what is it?"

And Zeus told him.

That was why, two days later . . .

★★★

. . . Achilles arrived at the palace of Princess

33

Polyxena—all marble and flaming torches.[8] Very classy but smoky and cold on your bare feet.

A trumpet sounded as Achilles entered the great hall. Princess Polyxena sat on a couch and jammed her pretty fingers inside her pretty ears. That trumpet could be a real pain.

There were only two other people in the room that Achilles could see . . . one was dressed as a Trojan sergeant—the enemy! He stood in a shadowy corner, but Achilles knew that no common soldier would dare to attack him.

Next to the sergeant stood a strange, hunched figure in a cloak that could almost have been a very tall eagle. Achilles was sure that he could see a sharp, curved beak poking out from underneath its hood. Something about that figure made even Achilles shiver a little.

The trumpet stopped. "Thank god for that!" Polyxena sighed. "Now, you must be the famous Achilles?" she asked.

Achilles looked surprised. "No one else has this armor, made by the gods," he cried and looked as

---

8 The palace was all marble and flaming torches, not Achilles. I want you to picture the scene, so I have to put in parts like that. It's what writers do.

mighty as he could—you *know*, left hand on his heart, right hand stretched out waving around a heavy sword. "No one but Achilles has this armor that glows with the power of Mount Olympus."

"Oh, I don't know anything about armor," Princess Polyxena said with a giggle. "I'm more into dresses myself. Have you ever tried wearing a dress?"

A strange thing happened to Achilles. He seemed to shrink a little—like a hot-air balloon with a hole in it. His face turned red, and he couldn't look the pretty princess in the face. "Maybe," he mumbled.

Polyxena smiled a wicked smile. "I did hear something about you dressing up as a girl and pretending to be your sister. Is that right?"

"Yes," Achilles whispered.

"Your mom dressed you up as a girl so that you could escape from a battle without getting killed, didn't she?"

"Yes."

"Your mom really looks after you, doesn't she, Achilles? Saving your life in a battle by dressing you like a girl. Dipping you in the River Styx to stop you from getting hurt. Quite a mommy's boy, aren't you, Achilles?"

Silence.

"*Aren't* you, Achilles?"

"Yes."

"I couldn't hear you . . . the trumpets make me a little deaf. Say it again—louder."

"*Yes*!"

"Louder!"

"*YES*!"

Polyxena smirked. "Now, you've come here to ask for my hand in marriage," she said.

"A messenger said that you're crazy about me," Achilles said.

"And *are* you crazy about me?"

"You're very pretty," the warrior said and nodded.

"As pretty as Helen of Troy? A woman whose face can launch a thousand ships?"

"Prettier—they say her tired face could hardly struggle to launch seven hundred ships these days!" Achilles chuckled.

"Turn around," Polyxena ordered.

"What?"

"What? Has the trumpet made you deaf, too? I said, turn around. I want to see what you look like from the back," she said.

"The back?" he asked.

"Yes, you know—the side that isn't the front," she said impatiently. "Turn around."

Achilles turned. The princess leaned down and looked underneath her couch. "Right, Paris, fire the poisoned arrow!" she hissed quietly.

"Ooh!" came a groan from the gloom. "It's not easy, lying under here and trying to use my bow! And my hands are all numb and cold from lying on this marble floor."

"Get on with it!" Polyxena ordered.

There was a twang, and an arrow slithered out from under the couch. It skittered over the hard floor and hit the trumpeter on the toe. He gave a small gasp and fell to the floor with a clatter of the brass trumpet.

Achilles looked over his shoulder. "What was that?" he asked.

Polyxena waved a hand. "Nothing, Achilles. You've just had an arrow escape. Turn around, and *don't* look back unless I tell you." She ducked her head under the couch and said, "It'll have to be the poisoned dagger, Paris. Get him."

"Ooh! I'm so stiff. I bet I catch my death of a cold after this."

"Get *ON* with it!" Polyxena moaned.

Paris crawled out and wiggled across the floor like a snake.

Zeus and the cloaked figure next to him became as still as the marble pillars in the hall. As still as the trumpeter. As still as his clattered and battered trumpet.

Paris reached the feet of Achilles, took a deep breath, and lashed out with the poisoned dagger.

Achilles raised his foot off the ground, half turned, and saw Paris looking up, with fear in his eyes. Achilles raised his sword to strike. He swayed. He sighed softly. He fell over backward.

His famous armor clanged like a bell, and his sword crashed like a cymbal. "God!" Polyxena cried. "That's worse than the stupid trumpet noise!"

Zeus turned to the hooded figure next to him. "There you are, Avenger. One gone, and one more to go."

"One more?" the creature hissed through its beak.

"Paris. We still need to make sure that *Paris* dies. Then this whole Trojan War can end, and we can all go home," Zeus explained.

"I have to hang around till Paris dies?"

"You may as well. Make sure that they both go down

to Hades in the underworld together—it's always nice to have some company in the underworld."

The Avenger tapped its foot, and its sharp eagle claws clattered on the marble floor. "What about your cousin Prometheus? You made it my duty to find him. To bring him back and chain him to the Caucasus Mountains." The Avenger was breathing quicker now. "To visit him every day and tear out his liver!"

"You have to find him first," Zeus reminded him.

"He was in a place called Eden City," the Avenger squawked. "Four thousand years into the future. I was so close to catching him. I *know* he'll return there. I *know* it. I have to go forward in time and find him."

Zeus sighed. "There's time enough for that later. For now, let's get Paris killed and get him and Achilles down to Hades."

"Then I will fly to Eden City," the Avenger spat.

★★★

Prometheus on his white wings saw a green-and-blue planet ahead of him. A small silver moon hung above it. "Home," he said with a sigh. "Maybe Zeus will forgive me."

FOUR

FLYING OVER EDEN CITY—1795

You'll remember that I was left in a runaway balloon, flying over East River City . . . you DO remember that, don't you? Pay attention if you don't. Over in Paris some people had flown free like that—people like the Roberts brothers—but usually they just put a sheep, a duck, and a rooster in the basket.[9] *We were the first humans to fly in our country.*

Pa stood at the edge of the basket and looked down. I know he was a showman and a bit of a crook, but I had to admire him then. He wore his top hat pulled down firmly on his thick gray hair so

9 It's true. Look it up in some dusty old history book. I can understand why they would send up a flying sheep. But why a duck? Ducks can fly by themselves. Those balloon pioneers were odd people. But on with the story . . .

40

that it didn't blow away. The long tails of his black coat and the red-and-white striped cravat whipped around in the wind . . . red, white, and black were the colors of the balloon, of course, and we always thought of them as "our" colors. Now we were going to die in "our" colors.

Yet Pa stayed quite calm in the rocking basket.

"We're going to die!" I cried.

He turned and smiled at me. "Yes, Nell, we are going to die some day."

"I mean *this* day! We're going to die very soon when we crash!" I shouted.

Pa thought about this carefully. "Maybe. Maybe not. We're still alive now, aren't we?"

"Yes, but . . ."

"Then hang onto hope, Nell—hang onto hope!"

My cheeks were cold, and I realized that there were tears running down them. I wiped them away angrily. If Pa wasn't going to panic, then I wasn't.

I looked over the side of the basket and down to East River City below. It was a very *neat* city. The fields were square patches of green and yellow, grass and corn. The parks had ponds and shady, tree-lined paths. The streets were straight, and the sea to the east was calm and sparkling.

The expressions on the upturned faces of the crowd were too small to see now, and wisps of clouds blew through the ropes that held the basket.

Pa threw some straw and wool into the metal firebox over our heads. "That'll make us go even higher!" I said. "We'll end up on the moon!"

"Better than ending up in the river," he said and laughed.

"What river?"

I moved quickly across to his side of the basket, and it rocked and almost tipped. Far below was a greasy, gray river, as sluggish as a slug and twice as cold. The east wind was carrying us over it now.

"This is the Eden river," he explained. "On the east bank is East River City."

"So we're heading for the west bank? What's there?" The cloud surrounding the balloon was blotting out the way ahead.

"Eden City," Pa said.

"Eden City?" I'd heard the name. We'd been to most of the big cities to give our shows but never to Eden City. "Why have we never been there before?" I asked.

"No one goes to Eden City," Pa explained. He sat down in the basket so that he was out of the clammy damp of the cloud. He unwrapped a small package of bread and cheese, and we shared it. With my cloth full of candy apples and sugar canes, we wouldn't starve. I smiled to think that those apple worms were probably the first worms in the world to fly into the clouds!

"Eden City is as far to the west as our people have gone. They built the city and tried to set off into the plains beyond. But they were stopped by the Wild People."

"Who are they, Pa?"

"The people who were here before we landed from Europe."

"They wouldn't be very pleased to see us, I guess?"

"No," he saïd and laughed. "They are wild! First they drove back the pioneers, who tried to make their farms on the plains. Then they headed for Eden City. They have lots of tribes and thousands of warriors. They all came together to surround Eden City."

"Then they must have captured it," I said. "If we land there, we'll be the prisoners of the Wild People!"

Pa shook his head. "Eden City built big wooden

walls to keep the Wild People out. The Wild People are surrounding Eden City—not many people can get in or out. A ship or two gets through with food. Just enough to keep them going. It's a siege, and it's been going on ten months now."

"They must be great fighters to keep out the Wild People," I said.

Pa made a face to show that he doubted it. "We have metal. We have guns, and we have bullets—the Wild People just have stone axes. Wooden bows and stone-tipped arrows. Eden City can't kill ten thousand wild warriors—but the Wild People can't fight musket fire. It's what they call a stalemate. The siege could go on for a long, long time."

"And that's where we're headed?"

"If we make it over the wide river," Pa said. I noticed that the air was clearer, and we were dropping down out of the clouds now.

That's when I saw Eden City for the first time. East River City was a patchwork quilt of green, gold, and autumn brown set in a brilliant blue sea.

Eden City was a pile of gray-brown sludge. Tall buildings rose like rotten teeth from blackened gums. Even in the autumn gale, a fog of grimy smoke hung over the place like a dirty blanket over a corpse.

"There's nowhere to land!" I told Pa as we slipped down into the gloom. "The streets are too narrow. The buildings are too high. We'll smash into them and die!"

"Stop talking about dying, Nell. Trust me—I'm a doctor," he said and reached for the handle over his head.

This time, I didn't argue with him about the "doctor" part of his name. He began pushing the lever backward and forward, and it creaked and huffed. "Bellows," he explained. "One of the greatest of the Roberts brothers' inventions. Inside the hot-air bag is a second bag. The second bag is filled with fresh air, which is heavier than hot air. So if I pump the bellows, I fill the inside bag with fresh air. We get heavier and come down in a controlled landing. See?"

"No."

He began again. "Inside the hot-air bag is a . . ."

"No. I mean I don't see how it helps us. We're still going to crash into one of the chimneys, be tipped out onto a roof, and fall into the street," I moaned.

"No, we're not," he said. "Trust me—I'm . . . an aeronaut!"

The balloon was falling faster now. We sped over the heads of men in canoes. They seemed to be wearing suits made out of animal skin and were carrying bows and arrows.

"Those are the Wild People," Pa said. "They're trying to stop supply ships from getting in and out of the harbor."

I just nodded. I could see sailing ships at the quayside now, deserted and rotting in the water. Their tall masts reached up to snatch at us and bring us down onto their decks.

"But where are we going to land? In the river?"

"On the waterfront," Pa said calmly.

We grazed the tip of one ship's mast, and it snapped off. The balloon basket tipped crazily, and I held onto the costume box at the bottom. Pa began pumping faster now, and we dropped even quicker.

People were gathering on the quayside and pointing up at us. I could hear their excited voices now. A horse screamed in fear and galloped off with the rider clinging onto its neck. Crows clattered, cawing into the air as we swept toward their roosts on the rooftops.

The window of a house opened, and a woman in a blue checked dress looked out. I'll swear that I could have reached out and shaken her hand.

We dropped down and brushed against the canopy of a grocer's, bounced into the air, and dropped back down to the level of the first-floor windows. Then we stopped. Suddenly.

Pa looked over the side. We were just above the ground—around head height to a tall man. The rope that held our wooden cannon had wrapped itself around the post of a gas lamp, and it held us fast.

The balloon tugged and strained at the rope, but it wouldn't budge. "Out, Nell!" Pa cried. "I told you that I'd get us down safely."

I jumped out of the basket and placed my feet on the rope that was holding us. I did my tightrope walk down to the lamppost, grabbed the post, and slid down it.

The crowds of people who had rushed to get a closer look couldn't help but clap.

Pa just leaned over the side of the basket and dropped to the ground. He looked at me with some disgust. "Show-off," he muttered and then turned and smiled suddenly at the crowd. "Ladies and gentlemen of Eden City," he cried. "Welcome to Dr. Dee's fabulous Carnival of Danger!"

The crowd clapped weakly, not sure just how they should greet a couple of strangers who had dropped from the sky.

Pa turned to me quickly. "Suckers! Look at them. Hundreds of them. Suckers! We'll make a fortune and then fly off!" He turned back to the crowd. "See Gregory the Great, all the way from Russia, fired from a cannon!"

"We left the net behind, Pa," I reminded him.

From the side of his mouth, he muttered, "I'll fire you into the rigging of the ships! It shouldn't hurt."

"Thanks."

"See Miss Cobweb from England dance the tightrope," he cried.

"We don't have a tightrope."

"You just walked down one from the balloon . . . and see Captain Dare dive into flaming water."

"We don't have the pool with us," I said.

"Dive into the river."

"It's filthy!"

"We'll make enough money to pay for a bath,"

he argued.

At that moment there was a murmuring in the crowd, and a small and weasel-faced man in a long black coat and blue dungarees pushed his way through. He had a silver star pinned to the coat and a brown mustache almost as wide as his broad shoulders. "Sheriff Spade!" a woman in a dirty green shawl said to her friend, who had even dirtier, even greener teeth.

"Make way for Mayor Makepeace!" Sheriff Spade called.

A fat man in a fine black suit followed him, and the crowd backed away, leaving the fat mayor standing alone in front of us. "Welcome to Eden City!" he cried.

Now, that was probably the last thing I expected to hear. We were used to being run out of town by angry lawmen who thought that we were just there to rob Pa's suckers.[10]

"I see that you bring us weapons for the fight against the Wild People outside our troubled walls,"

---

10   All right, we WERE just there to rob the suckers. But they could take care of themselves. There was no need to call in the law. You can feel a LITTLE bit sorry for us traveling show people!

the little sheriff said. Even his voice was a squeaky weasel voice.

"We have?" Pa asked. It was unusual to see Pa lost for words.

The mayor nodded at the cannon.

"But we need much more than that. We need new muskets, gunpowder, and bullets. We're getting desperately low."

The people in the crowd nodded gloomily.

"I'm sorry to hear that," Pa said.

The sheriff stroked his mustache and squeaked in a voice like a flute, "The worst thing about the Wild People is that they don't just kill you . . . they *scalp* you! They take all your hair off by peeling the skin away from the top of your head. It's horrible."

"You've seen it?" I gasped.

"No, but I've heard the tales," the sheriff said and shuddered. "Brrrr!"

"But now you've come to our rescue!" the mayor said and laughed his full-bellied laugh.

"We have?" I asked.

"You and your flying machine can bring us in all the supplies we need," he said. "You can buy them in East River City and fly them across. Our ships are trapped in port by the canoe warriors."

I could almost hear Pa's brain ticking, and his eyes darted around the crowd. "We'd need money to buy weapons," he said.

"We have all the money you need," the mayor said.

Pa's face split into a grin as wide as the Eden river. "That's a lot of money," he said and licked his lips.

The mayor waved a hand at a building behind him, as round and squat as a toad. "Let's put you up at the Storm Inn for the night, and you can set off tomorrow."

Pa put his arm around my shoulders and spoke from the corner of his mouth. "Of all the suckers in all the world, this has to be just about the biggest little sucker of them all."

"Great," I said with a sniff. "Out of one disaster and into another one, I'll bet."

FIVE

TROY—AROUND 4,000 YEARS AGO

Yes, back to where we started, but time has moved on a little. Except for Achilles, who was now dead. Death usually stops time moving on for most people. But Achilles was not "most" people . . .

Zeus sat on his cloud over the windy plains of Troy.[11] Hera smiled. This was rare. In fact, Zeus couldn't remember the last time she'd smiled. "This is *much* more fun," she said and chuckled. (He *could* remember the last time she'd chuckled. It was when he'd sat on a thistle on Mount Olympus.)

---

11   Troy is famous for two things—a wooden donkey and the wind. Don't ask me why it's famous for the wind, but it is. With this book, you don't just get a story—you get a weather forecast too at no extra cost.

"Yes, Troy has been too boring for too long. That's why I got Paris to kill Achilles."

"And *now* you've had Paris killed!"

"Ah, yes," Zeus said and nodded. "Killed in a battle on the windy plains of Troy. Shot with a poisoned arrow and died very slowly."

"Why are they called the windy plains?" Hera asked.

"Dunno," Zeus said with a shrug. "Just one of those things. Troy has windy plains like . . ."

". . . like Helen has a face that launched six hundred ships," Hera put in.

"I thought it was a thousand ships," Zeus said.

"She's not *that* good," Hera said and sniffed.

"And she was no help at all when Paris was wounded. That's why he sent for his first wife, Oenone. She was a great healer."

Hera snorted. "Ha! Paris ran off with Helen and then expected his ex-wife to heal him! I'd have refused."

"Oh, Oenone refused," Zeus said. "She just let Paris die. Then, *after* he was dead, she felt a bit ashamed, and she killed herself."

"Stupid woman," Hera sneered. "Still, it's good to see *something* happening down there. We created these humans for our pleasure. It's good to see some action. This siege is still pretty boring. Have you got a plan to end it?"

"I have . . ." Zeus began. He stopped and looked up at the sun. His godlike ears heard the sound of beating wings somewhere higher than the highest clouds.[12]

"Ah!" Hera cried. "It's your wicked cousin Prometheus." The rare smile slid off her face like ice off a penguin's back.

The white-winged god slowed his flight, circled the cloud, and landed gently beside the married gods. His face was tanned with the glare of countless billions of stars, and he looked weary. He slipped the wings off his back and stretched.

"Good day, cousin," Zeus said. "Have you completed the task I gave you? Have you found one true hero among those pathetic little humans?"

Prometheus (or Theus, as we came to know him) nodded slowly. "I went forward in time to search for a hero. I met some brave and bold people but never quite the perfect hero."

12   You will remember, if you were paying attention, that the gods had wonderful eyesight. I should have mentioned that they also had ears like bats . . .well, not pointy and hairy. I mean ears that could hear sounds that only bats (and gods) could hear.

"So you've failed?" Hera gloated.

"No," Theus said with a frown. "I just haven't succeeded *yet*."

"You *failed*!" she cried.

"Not exactly . . ."

"So *exactly* what have you done?"

"I've been searching as Zeus told me and . . ."

"FAILED!"

Theus turned a little red in shame and looked down at the timeworn sandals on his feet. He shuffled them. "Ah, but . . ."

"Failed, failed, *failed*!"

"But, but . . ."

"There is no such thing as a human hero. Zeus set an impossible task," Hera spat.

"Did I?" Her husband sighed. "Sorry, Theus."

"Gods can be heroes. Humans can't. They are too stupid and selfish," Hera explained.

Theus looked up, eyes gleaming. "You're wrong! I remembered Troy. There must be heroes in Troy!"

Hera turned sharply. "You had better hope that you are right," she said with soft menace. "You know what will happen if you are wrong?"

Theus nodded miserably.

"Tell me what will happen, Theus?" she teased cruelly.

"You know," the demigod mumbled.

"I know," she said and nodded. She licked her lips, as if she could taste his torment. "If you *can't* find a hero, then the Avenger will take you and destroy you. And it will serve you right. You deserve it for stealing fire from the gods and giving it to those creatures."

Zeus gave a small cough. "And the Avenger is on its way here now, Theus. I sent for it to take Achilles and Paris down to Hades in the underworld. So tell me quickly if you can name a human hero and save yourself."

The demigod took a deep breath. "Achilles?"

"He's dead!" Hera spat.

"I arranged to have him killed last week. Anyway, he was a half god," Zeus said and sighed.

"Paris, then?" Theus asked hopefully.

"He's dead too," Hera put in. "Clever Zeus had him done away with only yesterday. And he was a coward anyway! He was no hero." She rose to her feet and looked down on Theus with a look more poisoned than Paris' arrow. "No one—not even Zeus—can call off the Avenger. You're a fire thief, Prometheus, and you will NEVER find a human hero because one has never been born yet."

"*Yet*," Theus said and nodded. He looked up at her and smiled gently. "Then I'll go back to the future and find one. There is a temple in a place called Eden City. The humans call it the Temple of the Hero. I found it when I went there in the year they called 1858."

Hera looked furious. "If this hero has a temple, then he'll be dead. That doesn't count. You have to show Zeus a *live* hero."

Theus nodded. "I've thought of that. I'll go back to another year *before* he died. I'll find him and show him to Zeus *alive*."

Hera's mouth turned down at the corners as if she doubted that the plan would work. But her eyes had a cunning glint in them. "And which human year will you go back to?" she asked.

Theus rubbed his star-worn eyes and thought. "I'll go back a human lifetime . . . they live for three score years and ten. Seventy years before 1858 is . . . er . . . 1795!"[13]

---

13 Oh, yes, YOU know the answer should have been 1788. But there was no school on Mount Olympus—the gods thought that they knew everything. So, Theus would have failed all the math tests that you would pass. Don't feel sorry for him. He could fly beyond the farthest stars, which is much better than knowing how many tortoises make a dozen.

"So you will go to Eden City in 1795, will you?"

Theus nodded. Theus was a kind god who loved humans. He was brave and strong, honest, unselfish, and loyal. He kept his fingernails clean and always washed behind his ears. He was just the sort of person that you would want for a friend.

He could also be pretty stupid.

If you DID have him for a friend (as I did), then you'd have told him this: if you are on the run from someone who will grind you smaller than dust, you hide. And when you hide, you do NOT tell anyone where to find you.

In a word, TRUST NOBODY.[14] Zeus jumped to his feet, and the cloud swirled around his knees. "Wings," he said, and he cupped a hand to his ear. "Flying as fast as a shooting star. It's the Avenger, Cousin Theus. Better flee!"

Theus gathered his wings and strapped them on quickly. He launched himself over the edge of the cloud and hid beneath it just as the Avenger landed next to Zeus.

Then Theus let himself drift gently down toward

14 All right, that's two words, but you know what I mean.

Troy. The winds of the windy plains carried him silently out to sea. So silent that the Avenger couldn't hear him.

Once he was on the other side of Earth, he began to climb again. Beyond the clouds and past the moon. He left the planets behind and sped toward the stars. Out there, time was different. If you could fly fast enough and leave the planets behind in a blur, then you were racing ahead through time.

Theus was free and could have stayed there, safe for all time. But he missed those curious humans. He wanted to see Eden City again.

★★★

Zeus was in a good mood. He lay back on the cloud and looked at the feathered Avenger. Zeus could see it in all of its ugliness. YOU couldn't. No human could see its true shape. When it was flying, it looked like an eagle. When it was walking, it looked like a hunched man in a feathered, golden cloak with a beaked nose and glittering eyes. Its neck was slightly twisted, as if it had been broken once and never fixed properly.

"Well, Avenger, you seem to have failed to capture Prometheus," the god said.

The creature shifted from foot to foot, uncomfortable. "I will find him in time," it hissed.

"There's work to do in Troy first," Zeus said.

The Avenger sighed with a breath like the rattle of pennies in a tin can. "Achilles? His body has been burned. Now I have to take his spirit to Hades in the underworld, I suppose?"

"And Paris," Zeus said.

"Is he dead too?"

"Yesterday. Nasty accident with an arrow."

"Can't say that I'm sorry," the creature said and shuffled. "I never liked the sniveling little coward."

Zeus pointed toward the massive walls of Troy. "See them? Their ghosts are wandering around the walls wondering where to go."

The Avenger stretched its wings. "Avenger, dear!" Hera called. She smiled for the second time that day. "When you've done that small task, then come back and see me, will you?"

The creature nodded stiffly and then launched itself into a slow spiral glide toward the ghosts of Achilles and Paris.

They were arguing.

" . . . and I say it serves you right!" Achilles was

raging. "It's not even like you beat me in a fair fight. You had to hide under your sister's couch like . . . like a serpent. Then you wiggled out on your fat little belly."

Paris pouted. "My belly isn't fat."

"Not *now*, it's not," Achilles agreed. "But it *was* when you were alive. I don't know what Helen saw in you. A woman so lovely that her face could launch five hundred ships, and she runs off with a weedy worm like you!"

"It was a *thousand* ships, actually," Paris shouted, and the winds of the plains blew through him. "And you Greeks with your thousand ships *still* can't capture Troy. You never will."

"Want to bet?" Achilles said, and he would have said it through clenched teeth if he'd had any. He jabbed a finger at his enemy's shoulder, but it did no good. The ghostly finger passed through the ghostly shoulder and out the other side.

"Excuse me, gentlemen," a feathered figure interrupted. "Would you like to come with me?"

"You can see us?" Achilles asked, and he would have blinked if he'd had eyelids. "None of the others in the Greek camp or in the city can see us."

"I *know*," Paris groaned. "I went up to my ex-wife, Oenone, just as she was about to throw herself on my funeral fire, and I said to her, I said, 'Doesn't that jolly well serve you right?' And do you know that she acted like I wasn't there. I felt like *such* a fool!"

"You are a fool," Achilles snarled, and he'd have curled his lip if he'd had a lip.

"Now look here, Achilles . . ." Paris began.

The Avenger stepped between the two. "Paris, shut up. I am taking you away with me, and I don't want you squabbling like rats in a nest."

"Rats? It's been years since I tasted a rat," Paris said and sighed.

But Achilles had other things on his mind. "Where are you taking us, feathered fiend?"

"I am taking you to the god Hades in the underworld."

Paris would have rolled his eyes in horror if he'd had any eyes to roll. "Oh, hell!" he said.

"Exactly," the Avenger said, and he wrapped a wing around each dead warrior.

The ground seemed to open, and a long stairway led down into the darkness of the dead.

SIX

EDEN CITY—1795

You may remember that we left my story at the Storm Inn on the waterfront of Eden City. Mayor Makepeace and the people of that grim city seemed to think that we were the answer to their prayers. They were a city under siege— just like Troy. Now, just like Troy, they had a Helen there to join the fight. Me.

Pa enjoyed himself that night. He sat in the barroom of the Storm Inn and told tales of his daring deeds. The bar was crowded, and it seemed like everyone wanted to buy him a drink. I sat quietly in a corner and sipped a sarsaparilla. I'd spent an hour putting up our posters around the town, and it was thirsty work.

Now that the terror of the balloon ride was over,

I suddenly felt flat—a bit like the balloon, actually. And Pa's tales were all lies anyway.

"I was taught to fly by the Montgolfier brothers themselves. The Carnival of Danger was performing in Paris, and they came to see us. They wanted us to test their balloon for them. They'd sent up ducks and pigs, but no human being had ever had the courage to go up. They turned to us."

An old and toothless man leaned forward. "I saw your ad for that flying cannonball chap. I guess he went up . . ."

"Gregory the Great?" Pa laughed. "Greg wasn't so great that day. He doesn't mind being shot into a net, but the truth is, he is scared of heights. If he has to climb more than ten stairs to go to bed, he gets a nosebleed!"

The crowd laughed. The old man with no teeth sucked his thumb. His wife had even fewer teeth, and she sneered, "Stands to reason, you old buffoon. It's as plain as the nose on an elephant's face—it must have been that Captain Dare! If he can dive into a flaming pool from a tall tower, he must have had the nerve to go up in that there balloon—got to be braver than some pesky performing pig." Her rubber lips sprayed everyone at the table with spit when she tried to say "pesky performing pig." A lot of handkerchiefs wiped a lot of faces.

"Wrong!" Pa said with a laugh, and the old man gave his wife a nudge in the ribs as if his elbow was saying, "Not so smart, are you?"

A man as thin as a scarecrow called, "Don't tell us it was that Miss Cobweb, the tightrope walker? She'd be used to being up in the air. Don't tell us the first man in space was a woman?"

"Miss Cobweb did indeed offer to go up in the balloon," Pa said with a nod. There was a gasp from the audience, and the scarecrow man looked pleased with himself. "But I could not let her take the risk. No, sir, there was only one hero with the courage, the nerve, the guts, and the style to take on the mighty challenge . . ."

There was complete silence. You could have heard the beer drip off the dirty tables and onto the sawdust on the floor below. Pa looked around. He held the moment as long as he could. Then he spoke in a low voice. "The first man to fly free was none other than . . . Dr. Dee himself!"

"Ooooh!" the crowd breathed, as if they'd all been

holding their breath for 20 seconds—which they probably had.

The old man leaned forward. "Who's he?"

Pa looked a little angry. "*Me*, of course. The magnificent Dr. Dee himself. You, sir, have the honor of buying a drink for the greatest aviator that the world has ever known."

"You're an ape-y what?"

"A-vi-a-tor . . . a flier, a birdman."

"I haven't bought you a drink," the old man said.

"Then now is your chance!" Pa said, and the audience laughed. The old man got to his feet and shuffled to the bar. He counted a few coins from a thin wallet—his last coins by the look of it.

Pa looked at him as if to say, "Sucker." Sometimes Pa's greed could make him crueler than a north wind in the winter. I pushed through the crowd and thrust a bill into the man's shriveled hand. "Dr. Dee likes a joke—but he didn't really want you buying him a drink. Take this, and get yourself and your wife one too."

He looked at me through watery eyes. "Why thanks, Miss . . ."

"Miss Cobweb," I told him.

"My name's Waters," he said. "Thank you, Miss Cobweb."

"It's a pleasure."

I went back to my sarsaparilla and another hour of Pa's tall tales. When a distant clock clanged midnight, Sheriff Spade pushed open the doors of the saloon and called, "Right, folks, it's closing time. Get on home before I have to lock you all up!"

The crowd grumbled but rose with a clatter of chairs and stools and shuffled out into the night.

The sheriff walked up to Pa and spoke in a low, quick voice. "Listen, Doctor, as the sheriff I really should have the best musket that money can buy. How much would that cost me?"

"Twenty dollars," Pa said quickly.

The sheriff smiled and pulled out a wallet. "Is that all? I expected to pay twice as much!"

Pa almost choked on his beer. "Ah—oh—ooh!" he blustered. "You mean you want a quick-loading, flint-action, oak-butted Saracen Special?"

"I . . . I guess so."

"Then you are talking around sixty dollars," Pa said.

The sheriff's face fell. "That much?"

Pa took the wallet from his hand and looked through it. "You have fifty dollars here, eh? Tell you what," he said, sliding out the bills. "I may be able to give you a special deal—you being a lawman and all. I'll get you one for just fifty dollars. Don't tell everyone, or they'll all want one!"

Sheriff Spade looked worried. "That would never do. *I* have to be the only man in town to have the best musket."

Pa wrapped an arm around the lawman's shoulder and guided him to the door. "Don't worry, Sheriff. I may lose a little money on the deal, but I'll do it because I like you."

"You do?" the surprised sheriff said.

"I do."

"No one else does!"

"They *will* when you own a Saracen quick loader. They'll all look up to you." Pa placed a hand between the little man's shoulders and pushed him gently into the night. He tucked the money into an inside pocket. "Everyone's a sucker," he told me.

"Can you really get him a Saracen quick loader that cheap?"

Pa screwed up his face in pain. "Ohhhh! Nell!

You disappoint me. I thought you'd know me better than that." He held up a fist and counted off the plan on his fingers. "One, there is no such thing as a Saracen quick loader. Two, once we get out of here, we will not be coming back with a supply of guns. We will simply take the money and fly. If every sucker in town pays up as easy as the sheriff, then we will make a fortune, Nell, a *fortune*."

Pa had pulled some pretty mean stunts in his time, but this was the biggest. "We'll never get away with it," I said.

"Trust me—I'm a doctor. We'll be rich."

I shook my head. "But these people are under siege. If the Wild People attack and the people of Eden City have no guns, they could all be killed. You're not just robbing them. You're betraying them!" I argued.

Pa looked uncomfortable. "They don't need any more guns to hold off an army of men with stone axes and arrows. The Wild People will soon get tired of the siege and go away. They need to move to their winter camps in the south soon. You'll see. This is almost *too* easy," he said with a smirk.

Of course, *nothing* is *ever* that easy. There is always

a catch. But I didn't know what it was till I rose from the flea-ridden mattress and left the damp Storm Inn bedroom the next morning.

Fat Mayor Makepeace was sitting at a table with Pa chewing on some coarse bread and smelly cheese. "Eden City food isn't that good," the mayor was saying, "but once you're back with those guns, we'll drive off the Wild People and live like lords. And *you*, Dr. Dee, will be treated like the greatest lord in the city—why, they may even put up a statue of you . . . right behind mine!"

Pa smiled. "I look forward to that," he said. "Now, do you have the order and the cash? Two hundred dollars should get you all the weapons the town needs." The mayor took out a scroll of paper and passed it across the table. "Will your balloon carry all these guns?"

"Sir," Pa said, "in tests in Rome this balloon lifted an elephant off the ground."

"I thought you said it was tested in Paris," the mayor reminded him.

"It was, dear sir, but we traveled all over Europe before we came to this far-flung continent," Pa lied.

The narrow eyes flickered quickly, and the voice

lowered to a mouse squeak. "Sorry, doc, but I have to tell you that there are one or two of the citizens of Eden City who . . . er . . . are a little worried."

Pa sat back in surprise and raised one eyebrow. "Worried?"

The mayor placed a heavy bag of cash on the table. "Worried that you may take the money, fly off, and never come back."

Pa didn't even show a flicker of surprise that his plan had been discovered. "So . . . they want me to take you with us? There's no room in the basket. Not by the time we load all these guns," he added, with a flick of his long fingers on the list.

"No, they don't want you to take me with you—you wouldn't get me up in one of those newfangled monsters. No. They want you to leave the cannon behind."

Pa nodded. Suddenly, the mayor turned his blob of a nose in my direction. "They also want you to leave the girl behind."

I gasped. "They can't do that, Pa!"

Pa held up a hand. "An insurance policy for you, a willing hostage, I'm sure we understand. Little Nell is the dearest thing to me in all the world . . . dearest except for one thing . . ."

"One thing?" I asked.

"One thing?" the mayor echoed.

"One thing. My honor. If I leave Eden City and promise to return, then all the Wild People in the world would not keep me from coming back. My promise is stronger than the hardest steel. My word is as true as the aim on a Saracen rifle. I do not *need* to leave little Nell here."

The mayor chewed on a tough piece of bread and sucked on a grain that was stuck between his teeth. "The girl stays, or the deal is off."

Pa spread his hands. "A thankless public is sharper than a serpent's tooth, as Will Shakespeare said."[15]

"Did he?"

"Almost. I am deeply hurt by your suspicion. But, when I think about it, it is better if I leave Nell here."

"It is?" I cried.

"Why, yes. The less weight I have to carry, the more powder and bullets I can carry back from East River City. And as I *do* plan to return, you are not really a hostage at all!"

---

15 Pa had been an actor before I was born. He said that being a showman was not that much different.

"I'm not?"

"No, Nell, my dear. You need a little rest. A day or two in Eden City will do you no harm."

"But . . ." I began to object. Pa gave me a warning look and a small sign with his hand to stay quiet. "But . . . I'll miss you, Daddy dear!" I sniffled. (Pa wasn't the only one who could put on an act.)

"It won't be for long, dearly beloved child. While I am in the sky looking down on East River City, your dear mother will be up in heaven looking down on you! Protecting you while I am gone."

"She's not de . . ." I began to say but gave a little choking cough and tried again. "She's not de-cided to join the angels and forgotten me?"

"A mother's love will never die," Pa said and sighed.

The mayor blew his nose with a grubby handkerchief and then dabbed at a tear with the same stained rag. "A mother's love will never die. Did Shakespeare say that too?"

"No," Pa told him. "I did." He swept up the bag of money and smiled. "Good day, Mayor Makepeace. We leave in an hour."

The mayor rose slowly to his feet. "But the wind's

still from the east. If you go up now, you'll get blown *farther* east. You'll get blown straight onto the plains and to the camp of the Wild People! We find, in these parts, that the wind swings around to the west in the evening. Can you fly at night?"

Pa's eyes narrowed. "Even better," he said. "Even better. We leave tonight!"

"We?" the mayor asked and looked at me.

"Er . . . I mean *I* leave tonight!"

The mayor nodded and left us alone in the barroom. I could see myself trapped, like that other Helen, in Troy and under siege. Well, not exactly like that other Helen—because I was prettier, and she had had Paris for company. I would be all alone.

"Pa," I said, "you're not *really* going to leave me behind, are you?"

"Don't be stupid, Nellie. Of course I'm not."

"The name is Nell," I said.

SEVEN

THE UNDERWORLD—4,000 YEARS AGO

I don't know what the underworld is like. You have to be dead to go there.[16] *But I've heard the tales, so you'll have to trust me when I tell you that it is NOT the sort of place you would go for a picnic. It's not even a place you'd go to on a school field trip, and they are usually bad enough. No, the underworld of the gods was nastier than Mayor Makepeace's handkerchief.*

Achilles and Paris trudged down the gloomy corridors, and the scent of death would have filled

16 Some smart reader is going to say, "Aha! There was ONE living man named Orpheus who went down to the underworld to snatch his dead girlfriend back. In the end he failed and was torn into little pieces by a bunch of wild women." All right, I know about Orpheus. The point is that I'm not Orpheus, and MOST people are dead when they go there.

their nostrils . . . if they'd had nostrils.

"I'm glad I haven't got any nostrils," Paris muttered.

"Are you going to complain all the way to the underworld?" Achilles asked.

"No. I'm just saying that this is not a pleasant place."

Achilles turned to him and glared fiercely. "We wouldn't BE here if it wasn't for your stupid little trick."

The Avenger stopped and turned. "I have warned you not to argue. You annoy me. And if I am annoyed, I will tell the great god Hades of the underworld to think of some new and nasty tortures for you."

Paris would have raised his eyebrows . . . if he'd had any.[17] "My dear old chum Achilles. How nice it is to have you for company. Enemies in life but best of pals after death."

"Eh? Oh, yes! I look forward to spending some time chatting about out lives in Troy. It was a tough battle, but it gave us heroes a chance to show the world what we're made of."

The Avenger hissed. "No need to overdo it."

---

17 Look, can I drop this "if he had any" stuff? They are ghosts. They have no bodies, so they can't do the things that humans can do. But now that you have the idea, I can save my pen and ink and let you add "if he had any" in all the right places. Agreed? Good. Now I want to get back on the road to the underworld. That's my intention.

He led the way down a path cut into warm rock. Warm but damp, so it steamed a little. "Not long now to the Styx," it said.

"Oh, the Styx! That's where my mother dipped me when I was a baby," Achilles said.

"You have to pay Charon, the ferryman, one obol each to get across," their eagle-shaped guide told them.

"I don't have any money!" Achilles cried. "Money's no use on a battlefield."

"Don't worry," Paris told him. "I've got plenty. I had loads of loot in Troy. The trouble is, there was nothing to spend it on. To be honest, I'm glad to be out of that miserable place."

"It wasn't a lot of fun on the windy plains," Achilles said.

"What was it like?"

"Windy."

The Avenger made a grating sound that could have been a laugh. "Once you get to the underworld, you may change your mind. You may be begging to go back to Troy!"

The warriors stopped. "We're going to a land of heroes—the Islands of the Blessed—aren't we?" Paris asked.

The Avenger gave the same laugh again. "Is that what you think?" It turned its glittering eyes on the ghosts. "When you cross the Styx, you come to the Asphodel Fields. That's where ordinary humans wander around as ghosts. But you are NOT ordinary humans. You are killers!"

"Warriors!" Achilles objected.

"You will pass on to the next level of Hades and be taken to Tartarus. I'm sure Lord Hades will think of some suitable punishment for you!"

"Punishment? What sort of punishment?"

The hunched shoulders of the Avenger hunched a little more in a shrug as it walked on. "There's Tantalus down there. He is starving and thirsty. He stands in a lake up to his neck in water. But if he bends to drink, the water dries up. He stands with the branch of a fruit tree over his head. If he tries to reach for the fruit, then the branch is blown up out of his reach."

"Nasty," Paris muttered. "I don't like the sound of that. What did he do to deserve that?"

"He gave the food of the gods to the humans," the bird shape sneered.

"Ah," Achilles said and nodded. "Just as Prometheus

was punished for giving fire to the humans!"

The Avenger stopped sharply again. Now its voice was as harsh as sharp steel on living bone. "Do NOT remind me of Prometheus. As soon as I've disposed of you two, I will seek him out and destroy him completely. He will not escape. If it takes forever, I will make him wish that he had never been born. Hurry! Hurry! I want to get back on his scent!"

The ghosts hurried.

"I thought that the underworld was a pleasant place," Achilles grumbled.

"The people who lived good lives take the fork to the right and end up in the Elysian Fields—they're full of people dancing and singing," the Avenger explained. "Some people return from there to the world above—if they die and return to the Elysian Fields three times, they spend the rest of time in the Islands of the Blessed, where sorrow is banished."

"I like the sound of that!" Paris cried. "Any chance we might get there?"

"Yes. Fat chance," the big bird spat. "Now here we are at the River Styx. Step into it."

A wide and lifeless river stretched out before them. It didn't glint and shimmer like an earthly river. Down there, even the daylight was dead.

"I thought we had to pay to ride the ferry with Charon," Paris said. "I've got my obols ready."

"Step into the Styx, and you will have new bodies when you step out. We cannot torture you if you don't have a body."

The bird spread its wings, and the heroes fell backward into the river of poison. They came up spluttering and swimming for their lives . . . or were they swimming for their deaths?

They struggled out and onto the shore, where the Avenger waited.

But the war heroes weren't looking at it. Their jaws dropped (now that they *had* jaws). Their eyes were fixed on the monster that stood in front of them next to the Avenger.

"What in Hades is that?" Paris breathed.

The creature was roughly human. But its body was almost square. It had to be. Along the top edge of the square sat its 50 heads. Down each side of its body were 50 arms.

The Avenger said, "Meet the Hecatonchires."

"Hello, boys!" the 50 heads called. That would have deafened the ears of the heroes, but the air of the underworld deadened even the loudest noise.

Paris waved a few fingers and said, "Hello, Hec!"

Achilles stood with his feet and arms apart like a wrestler ready to do battle with the monster. "I am the mighty Achilles. Come, monster, do your worst!"

"Ohh! Doesn't he talk funny?" Head 35 said. The other heads agreed that he talked very funny. "A bit like that Hector we had down here last month," Head 3 said, and again the other heads agreed. "Still, you know what we say?" Head 14 cried, and all the heads joined in. "The bigger they come, the harder they fall!" And 50 heads laughed together while 100 arms clapped against the monster's sides.

"Choose your weapon, creature from hell!" Achilles cried, and the heads giggled.

"Oh! Creature from hell, eh? Well, sticks and stones may break my bones . . ." And the other heads joined in, ". . . . but names can never hurt me!"

Achilles turned purple with rage, while Paris just looked a little worried. "Choose your weapon!" Achilles roared, but his voice fell dead on the dark rocks and pebbles at the edge of the poisoned river.

"Stones!" Head 3 said. "We choose stones," and the third pair of arms waved at the stones by the shore.

Achilles swooped down and picked up a stone. Then the Hecatonchires stretched down to its right, and each of the 50 right hands grasped a stone.

But the weight was too much even for its massive legs. As the monster tried to straighten up, it wobbled and then toppled onto its side, and the stones fell with a dull clatter to the shore. The Hecatonchires struggled to its feet. "Sorry, kid," Head 35 said. "That always happens!" Head 3 put in, and the other heads said, "Always."

Paris stepped forward. "Your trouble is that you're not using your brain."

"*Brains*!" Head 14 reminded him.

"*Brains*, then," Paris said and nodded with his single head. "You should lean to the right and pick up five stones, say. Then you lean to the left and pick up five stones in your left hands. Five at a time. Ten times to the left, ten to the right, and you're fully loaded. That way you stay balanced, don't you?"

"I suppose he has a point there," Head 35 said. "We can try it," Head 3 suggested. "Yes, try it," the others joined in.

At first it was a slow job rocking right and then left.

"Left . . . two–three–four–five . . . and right . . . two–three–four–five!" it rocked. "Left . . . two–three–four–five . . . and right . . . two–three–four–oops!"

Paris clapped his hands happily. "It works!"

Achilles groaned. "You need to borrow one of the monster's brains because you seem to have lost yours!"

"I have? Why?"

Achilles just shook his head wearily.

Some stones were dropped. Head 17 swore a very nasty word that shocked the others. But after a while the monster got into a "left . . . two–three–four–five . . . and right . . . two–three–four–five!" rhythm, and soon 100 rocks were clutched in 100 hands. "Righty-ho! Ready when you are," Head 35 said to Achilles. Achilles pulled back his arm and threw his rock. It smacked into the nose of Head 25, and the head roared.

A moment later 100 rocks rained down on Achilles. His armor was crushed like a snail's shell under a horse's hoof. His new body was mangled and twisted, broken and battered. A blood-soaked head in a shredded helmet stuck out from the pile of stones. Paris removed a rock from Achilles' mouth, and his new teeth tinkled to the ground.

"Are you all right?" the prince of Troy asked.

"Wa-waaaah? Waah-wah waaaah wah . . . wa-wah!" Achilles said in a spray of blood from his broken lips.[18]

"I only asked," Paris said.

"Wow!" the Hecatonchires gasped with at least 40 of its heads. Head 35 said, "It works really well, doesn't it? Now that we know how to load up, we'll be unbeatable!"

Achilles' body healed quickly—after all, he was immortal; he had a new body that could be hurt and bent out of shape but never destroyed. New teeth slid out of the empty gums, and the flesh healed without a scar. He pushed off the pile of stones and rose shakily onto his mended legs. "If we'd had a creature like that in Troy, we'd have won in ten minutes, not more than ten years."

"Just as well you didn't," Paris said and laughed.

Achilles glared at him through his even-newer eyes and was about to hiss something through his even-newer teeth. But he stopped. He grabbed Paris by the arm and dragged him away from the Avenger.

18 Of course, you don't need me to tell you what that means. You do? Very well. It means, "All RIGHT? What do you think, dummy?"

He whispered so low that not even the eagle ears of the bird caught the hero's words. "We can't stay in this awful place. I've got a plan to get us out of here. Just back me up and agree with me . . . no matter how odd it sounds."

"Yes," Paris said and nodded.

"Yes, what?"

"Yes, I'm agreeing with you. You told me to."

Achilles wondered if his old enemy would make a very useful friend, but he turned to the Avenger anyway. "Avenger!"

"What is it, Achilles? I'm in a hurry."

"I know. You want to go after that evil Prometheus."

"That's my business."

"No! It's everyone's business. You can't have a dangerous demigod like that on the loose," Achilles said.

"I agree," Paris said.

"That's why the gods have an Avenger like me." The bird snapped and clacked its beak.

"And you are treated so badly by the gods. They sent you out to do an impossible task. Even if you find Theus, you'll struggle to hold him on your own."

The Avenger felt its twisted neck and knew that it

was true. "Perhaps," it said.

"You need a few true heroes to help you."

"I do," the bird said. "Zeus expects me to do everything. Chase Prometheus through space and time and then stop to take heroes to Hades."

"It's SO unfair," Achilles said with a sigh. "I wouldn't blame you if you got some expert help."

"Pah! There is no expert like me," the Avenger said, and its beak rose proudly in the air.

"I agree, but a few heroes would be useful . . . someone like me and Paris."

"Yes, I could use a few good men . . ." The Avenger nodded.

"And a monster," Head 17 of the Hecatonchires put in. "Especially now that I've learned how to throw a hundred rocks at the same time!"

The Avenger almost had a smile on its beak. "I promised Zeus that I'd take you to Hades, Achilles . . . but I didn't say *when*. After we've caught Prometheus, I can always bring you back here, can't I?"

"You could," Achilles said carefully and shook his head at Paris, who was going to say, "Not if I can help it!"

"But Zeus would never give me the extra wings

that you'd need," the Avenger said with a sigh.

"His wife, Hera, might," Achilles said. "She doesn't like Paris much, but she likes me."

The Avenger's savage eyes looked deep into Achilles' eyes. "I'll take you with me," it said.

"And me?" Paris asked.

"And me?" Head 35 asked.

"Yes. Together we will capture the Fire Thief, and I will destroy him! Destroy him!"

★★★

Prometheus had reached the farthest stars again, and time had ticked forward enough. He headed for Eden City in 1795.

EIGHT

EDEN CITY—1795, THE DAY AFTER WE ARRIVED

Have you ever had this really creepy feeling that things keep happening to you—things that you have no control over? As if someone was pushing you around like a pawn on a chessboard? The way that things came together that day seemed normal at the time. But, looking back, I can see that a weird "Fate" was making things happen. So, if you don't believe in fate, you won't believe what happened next. Take this book back to the store or library. Get your money back. Do NOT read on!

Prometheus drifted down on his wide white wings toward the ugly smudge by the river that was Eden City.

He'd been there once before, in the future.[19] At that

88

time the city had been covered by a cloud of purple and yellow, green and brown, gray and black. Twisting towers and sharp spires had risen out of the mist.

Now, in 1795, the city was smaller, and a wooden wall had been built around it to cut it off from the living plains of waving grass. Eden City stood there like a dark wart on a beautiful face.

The buildings were not so high in those days, but they were rotting and dank, the streets dark and snaking and puddled and muddied.

Theus hung in the air and saw a bright flash of yellow flames explode below him. Then there was a hiss, and a lump of lead flew through his arm.

The (half-)godly ears heard a man far below cheer, "I got it! I hit that big bird! It'll feed the family for a week! I got it!" Theus saw that it was an old man who was as twisted as an Eden City street.

A sour-faced old woman cackled, "Fool! If you hit it, then why hasn't it fallen? You couldn't hit a barn

19   Yes, I know that doesn't seem to make sense. You can go to a place that you've been to in the PAST but not to a place that you've been to in the FUTURE. But Theus was a time traveler. He had been to Eden City in 1858 when it was even grimier and uglier than it was when I was there. Sounds unlikely, I know. But I have lived so long, and I am so old! We're ALL time travelers—it's just that most of us move forward. Theus could move both ways.

if you were standing inside it. You've just wasted precious powder that we could have used against the Wild People!"

"I was sure I hit him," the man said, sighed, and moved back toward the shabby shack that the couple called home.

"Why don't you do something useful?" the woman demanded. "Go out and rob some poor stranger."

"If they're poor, they're not worth robbing!" the old man grumbled.

"You *know* what I mean. Now, you go out stealing. I have to get back to the baby farm."

Theus shuddered. He'd given these humans fire. They used it to make choking smoke. They'd learned to use it to kill. "It was never meant to be like this," he said with a sigh and rubbed his wounded arm. It was already beginning to heal. "Maybe Zeus was right. Maybe the humans *are* too simple to be given fire. Maybe it's true that I should be punished for it."

Even a great demigod can get gloomy from time to time.

Theus looked down at the people hurrying below. Mostly he could see bent backs as the Eden City citizens looked down at their feet to make sure that they didn't step into something too disgusting. Only the bird hunter had been looking up.

There was one girl that Theus spotted who didn't hurry. She seemed to be wandering around like a stranger. Her hair was reddish-brown, and her face was lovely enough to launch a thousand ships. In fact, she was the loveliest girl you could wish to see in Eden City . . . ever.[20]

I was drifting through the streets, just passing the time till it grew dark and it was time to leave. Pa had told me that he would NOT be leaving me behind. He said he had a plan . . . but he would tell me at supper.

To stop me from moaning, he sent me out to prepare our escape. "We need a clear space in this crowded city to lay out the balloon and get it ready to fill with smoke. And then we need at least one strong man to carry the balloon along to that clear space. Off you go."

20 Yes, all right, so this beautiful girl was ME. I know you'll think that I am telling a small lie here, but I never saw a prettier girl in Eden City in the time I was there. No, honest, I REALLY didn't. I can tell that you don't believe me, but I don't care.

"What will you be doing?" I asked him.

"Resting . . . I need to be awake tonight if I'm going to fly the balloon back over the river to East River City." Then he climbed the stairs to his Storm Inn bedroom and left me to explore the city alone.

No one smiled or said hello to a stranger in Eden City. No one smiled, period. The windows of the houses and stores were clouded with grime. I'm a curious sort of person—I like to see the way people live. So I wandered through the streets peering into the grimy windows.

The stores didn't have much food—because of the siege, I guessed. And the clothes gathered dust on the racks since Eden City people were too stingy to buy new ones.

Horses and a cart or two rumbled past, and you had to jump out of the way. The wooden sidewalks creaked and tripped you. I thought that was why Eden City people walked with their heads down but looked quickly from side to side.

I suppose I was wrong. There was another reason why they looked around nervously, as if their lives depended on it. The reason was . . . their lives depended on it. But I was a stranger. I didn't know.

I passed one house that looked dirtier than the rest and wondered what went on inside.

The front was as faded and dirty as the rest of the houses. But this one had a bright red sign on the door. In yellow-gold letters it said, "Mrs. Waters' Wonderful World for Children. The Nicest Nursery in Town."

I squinted through the window. The bare wooden floor was covered in cradles. Some were so still that the spiders had woven their webs around them like some Sleeping Beauty bed.

A woman sat and looked at one cradle and rocked it. One child whimpered, and another coughed. But the round-shouldered, gray-shawled, stick-thin woman ignored them. Her eyes were fixed on *one* baby. She spooned some milk from a cup and fed it to the baby with a cooing sound.

She seemed to sense my eyes on her back and turned around with a face that was ax-sharp, ax-hard. It was a face that I'd seen in the Storm Inn the night before.

I moved away quickly down the dull street, past the dim alleyways, looking for somewhere wide enough to take our balloon. But I was looking ahead. I wasn't looking down the alleys. That's when I found out why the people of Eden City looked from side to side all the time.

There was danger in the darkness—even in the daylight dimness, thieves lurked. One waited till I'd passed the murky opening and then stepped out behind me. His hard hand wrapped itself around my throat and dragged me back into the passageway between two windowless walls. "Give me your money, or I'll cut your throat."

It was an old, twisted hand on an old and twisted man.

I've been in rough towns before, and Pa taught me how to deal with people like this. "Let go of my throat, or you'll choke me and never get my money," I croaked. He loosened his grip but held onto my jacket. I turned to look at him. It was the toothless old man I'd bought a drink for last night at the Storm Inn. I'd felt sorry for him!

Pa's advice was, "Confuse the suckers."

"Have you got any change?" I asked.

"You what?"

"I don't have any change. I just have bills. Tell me how much you want, and let's see if you have the change."

"Why . . . I have fifty cents," he said.

"Show me."

He struggled to hold my jacket in one hand and fumbled in his pocket with the other. He pulled out some change and showed it to me.

I picked out half of the coins.

"Now, I have no change at all. So add nothing to fifty cents, and you have fifty cents. Half of fifty is twenty-five, yes?"

"Yes."

"I take twenty-five cents and leave you twenty-five cents. We both have twenty-five cents, and everyone is happy!"

"Ye-es!" he said with a frown and let go of my jacket.

You won't believe what happened next.[21]

There was a rustle of feathers, and a huge shape dropped from the gray sky into the grayer alleyway. A man with white wings strapped to his back landed

---

21 But I'll tell you anyway. You want to know, don't you? Or maybe you want to guess. Go on. Guess. I made a run for it? Nope. He saw that he'd been tricked and called out, "Stop, thief!"? Nope. See, you'll have to see what I was going to tell you anyway.

behind the old robber. He was a large young man with skin the color of bronze and muscles as smooth and swollen as our balloon.

His face was as handsome as my face is beautiful. His hair was a little too long and girlie, but no one's perfect. He reached forward and picked up the robber by the collar of his ragged jacket. "I saw him trying to rob you," the stranger said. He was dressed in a light sleeveless tunic and no pants. Must have been cold, I thought.

I suppose you'd have fallen to the floor in a faint. What would that get you? Muddy clothes.

I'd been to weird places and seen weirder sights in our travels. It wasn't long since I'd dropped out of the sky myself. So I guess I wasn't as shocked as I should have been. I may have blinked . . . once.

"How did you see us?" I asked.

"I was flying over the city," he explained.

"On those wings?" I asked.

"There's no other way to fly," he said.

"I use a balloon myself," I said.

"A what?"

"We use fire to make smoke and lift a big bag in the air," I told him.

His face brightened. "Ah, so you humans have found one good use for fire. I'm pleased."

"I'm pleased that you're pleased—but will you put down the old man before you choke him to death?" I pleaded.

He dropped the thief into the damp dust. The old man staggered and seemed lost. He looked at us. "Been nice meeting you," he said and smiled his toothless smile. He jingled the coins in his hand. "My wife will be pleased with this twenty-five cents," he said with a dazed and glazed look in his eyes as he wandered, wobbling, into the main street.

"I'm Theus," the large stranger said.

"I'm Helen," I said and held out a hand to shake.

I'll swear that his bronze skin turned a lot paler when I said that.

"Who?"

"Helen. Never heard the name before?"

"Oh, yes," he murmured. "But that was in Troy."

"Is that beyond East River City?" I asked.

"Way beyond," he said.

"Look. My pa is looking for a strong man to help us. Want to come back to the Storm Inn with me?" I asked. Then I looked around me. "If I can find my way back. This city is like a maze—a maze made of water that shifts every time you move."

He nodded. "Eden City is like a living thing," he agreed. "You should have seen it when it grew bigger in 1858!"

"Huh?"

"Never mind. The Storm Inn is this way," he said, pointing in the opposite direction that I'd have gone. At the time I guessed that he'd seen the Storm Inn when he was flying over.

He slipped off his wings and tucked them under his powerful arms and then set off toward the waterfront district.

I followed.

NINE

ANCIENT TROY—4,000 YEARS AGO . . . BUT
LATER THAN THE LAST TIME WE WERE THERE

*Now you see how the different parts of the story are coming
together? If I was a fiction writer, then that's just the way
I'd make it happen. But, of course, I'm not a fiction writer
because this story is true. I'm telling you what happened to
me more than 60 years ago. But the tale of the Avenger,
the heroes, and the Hecatonchires hasn't come together with
Theus and I—yet. Be patient, dear reader. Be patient!*

Zeus had gone down to the windy plains again. He
was disguised as a wise old Greek man, and he was
going to meet the Greek leader Agamemnon. He
told Hera about his plan.

"I'm going to persuade the Greeks to build a

huge, hollow horse made out of wood that stands on wheels. They are going to fill it with soldiers and leave it on the plains," he said. "The Trojans will take the wooden horse into the city, and the Greeks will rush out to massacre all of them."

"It'll be a bit windy, won't it?" Hera argued. She could see a clever idea forming, and she was annoyed. Why hadn't she thought of it? Zeus would be *so-o* pleased with himself if the idea worked. He would boast about it for the next ten years.

"The Greeks will be nice and snug inside that horse, believe me," Zeus said.

"No, they won't," Hera sneered. "Those humans use something that we gods don't need," she reminded her husband. "Something called a bathroom. And if they don't use the bathroom, it can get very, *very* smelly inside a horse."

Zeus was annoyed at this fault in his plan. "They'll just have to go before they get inside the horse."

Hera the sneerer gave a little snort. "Carry on. Tell me why the Trojans would take this wooden wonder into their city?"

"The rest of the Greeks . . . the ones NOT inside the horse . . . will get into their ships and sail away.

The Trojans will think that they've given up and gone home. They will open the gates and take the wooden horse inside the city!" he cried.

"Why should they?"

"Because they will think that it is a holy Greek statue. They will take it as a prize of war," he said.

"No, they won't. If they see a big wooden horse, they'll say, 'Oh! Look! A big wooden horse!' Nobody in Troy will think it's a holy Greek statue," she scoffed. "No one will think of wheeling it into the city."

Zeus wiggled on the cloud over the city. "You could be right," he said.

"Zeus, I am *always* right. It's a crazy plan."

Zeus became angry and reached into a pouch on his belt and pulled out a thunderbolt. He threw it down to Earth in anger—and set fire to three Greek tents. The wind whipped the flames and singed the beards of the scattering, screaming soldiers. "Oops!" Zeus said. Then he turned to his wife and said, "Look, we are bored with this war. Have you got a better idea how to end it?"

Hera gave a small smile. "I'm glad you asked me that. I do. You go to the Greeks and tell them to build a huge, hollow horse made out of wood that stands on wheels. Then they fill it with soldiers. The Trojans will wheel it into the city."

She paused. Zeus glared at her.

She smirked. Zeus glared at her.

"Go on," she said. "Ask me."

"No."

"Go on. You want to know."

Silence. Suddenly, Zeus snatched a thunderbolt and hurled it at Troy. A few of the topless towers lost their tops.[22]

Zeus spoke quickly, like a sulky child. "Oh, very well then, you great-minded, great-mouthed goddess, and tell me *why* the Trojans will wheel the horse into the city."

Hera placed her hands calmly in her lap. "Because a spy named Sinon will go into Troy and *tell* the Trojans that this horse is a holy Greek statue. Sinon will *tell* the Trojans that it is a gift of peace from the Greeks who've gone home."

"And you think they'll believe it?" Zeus asked.

---

22 Oh, go on, argue. How can a tower with no top lose something that it doesn't have? That's what you're going to say. I know it. Well, listen. It was a famous playwright from England named Christopher Marlowe who said that Troy had "topless towers." He meant that they were incredibly high and the tops were lost in the clouds. See? Now, let's get on with it.

"They will."

"So where do I find this Sinon fellow?"

Hera shook her godly head. "No, Zeus. *You* simply disguise yourself as Sinon. It's easy for you to slip into the city and spread the word."

Zeus jumped to his feet and said, "I'll go and do it right now."

"Aren't you forgetting something?"

"Am I?"

"First you have to visit the Greek camp and get them to build the horse. It's only *after* the horse is built and the Greek ships have *left* that Sinon should go to Troy."

"Yes . . . I knew that," Zeus lied. "When I said I'll do it right now, I meant that I'd visit the Greeks with the horse idea."

The god smoothly changed his shape into that of a wise old Greek teacher and drifted down from the cloud to the edge of the Greek camp. A guard spotted him. "What is the password, stranger?" the guard called out.

"Let me through, or I will push a thunderbolt down your throat and roast you from the inside out," Zeus snarled.

The guard scratched his head. "That's not the password they told me."

"What did they tell you?" Zeus asked.

"They said the password was 'windy.'"

Zeus clapped his hands. "Well done, soldier. That is correct. The password is 'windy.' You have passed the test. I will tell your general Ulysses what a good guard you are," the god said as he walked into the camp.

The guard turned red with pleasure. "Why, thank you, sir. Thank you."

★★★

Later that day, as the sun set, Zeus was leaving Ulysses after explaining the trick with a wooden horse. "And you think it will work?" Ulysses asked, looking up at the half-finished statue that was as tall as the walls of Troy. The men were working on through the night by the light of bonfires that were whipped into sparks by the wind from the sea.

"It will work . . . just as long as you tell your men to go to the bathroom before they get inside the horse," Zeus said.

As Zeus crossed the plains, he wished that he could just fly into Troy. He didn't do a lot of walking—gods don't. His feet began to hurt, and he kept stepping on rusting swords, shattered armor, and squishy body parts that the burial troops had left behind. A battlefield can be a messy place. A ten-year-old battlefield can also be a very *smelly* place.

Ashes blew in his face from the funeral fire that had been built to burn the corpse of the hero Achilles. Zeus gave a grim smile as he brushed the ashes off his tunic. "You'll be tucked away in Tartarus by now, Achilles," he muttered and walked on toward the mighty walls of Troy. He headed for one of the secret gates that was so secret that everyone else had forgotten about it.

Night was falling, and Troy was in darkness.[23] But Zeus had the eyes of a god and could see his way clearly through the stone-paved streets and up to the palace of King Priam.

Behind the shutters of the darkened windows his sharp ears could hear sharper voices complaining. "Mom, I want a drink of water!"

"Shut up and go to sleep, or Hector's ghost will

23 "Aha!" you cry. "Of course it was in darkness if it was night!" But I mean that there were no candles or torches lighting the windows in the houses, streets, or topless towers. Candles are made from fat, and fat is precious food in a starving city. The candles had all been eaten. The Trojans went to bed early and left the streets in the moonlight—that's because they couldn't eat the moon, though they would have liked to. They believed that it was made out of cheese!

come and get you!"

"But, Mom, I can't go to sleep. All that hammering is keeping me awake! What is it, Mom?"

"The Greeks on the windy plains are building something."

"What are they building, Mom? Ladders to get in?"

"No. Mrs. Palamon next door says it's a big wooden model. Looks like it's going to be a dog."

"Wow! Mom, can I go on the walls tomorrow and take a look?"

"Only if you go to sleep now."

"Wow, Mom! The wooden hound of Troy! That'll go down in history, that will!"

"Sleep! Now!"

"Night, Mom."

"Nighty-night. Don't let the bedbugs bite."

"They tried, Mom, but I ate them. Night!"

"Night!"

Zeus walked on. He could hear the hammering too. But even his godly ears missed the soft grating sound of rocks sliding apart. A gateway from the underworld opened on the plains near the ashes of Achilles.

Hera, on the cloud over Troy, could see the gateway in the thin moonlight and the sparks from the Greek campfires. First an eagle head on a twisted neck appeared and looked around carefully. The enormous bird man stepped onto the sandy plains and made a sign for someone below to follow.

Achilles stepped into the silver light, and then came Paris. Finally a creature with 50 heads used 100 arms to pull itself aboveground. The gateway slid shut.

"Ugh!" Achilles gasped.

"Shh!" the many mouths hissed at him.

"But I just stepped in some ashes!" the hero complained.

"They're cold," Paris said. "They don't hurt."

"No . . . but they are the ashes of MY body!"

"Ugh!" Paris said and nodded.

"Shh!" the mouths hissed at him.

"Now wait here and stay quiet," the Avenger said.

"Shh!" the mouths hissed at him.

The creature clacked its beak, annoyed. "We don't want anyone to know that Achilles and Paris are back on Earth. Hera wants to see me. Wait here, and I'll be back before dawn. Then we'll set off in search of Prometheus."

Fifty-two heads nodded.

The eagle spread its wings and rose softly into the air, letting the dusty wind lift it toward the curious cloud.

Achilles nodded toward the walls. "There are a lot of guards on the walls tonight."

"They're looking at us, I think," Paris said.

"We need to get them to keep their heads down," Achilles said.

"Leave it to me," the 50-headed monster said softly.

The Hecatonchires wandered around the plains looking for rocks and put them into two piles on each side of its square body. Then it began to pick them up with a little chant—"Five to the left—five to the right—five to the left—five to the right!"— until its hands were full. "Hey! I didn't fall over!" Head 35 said with a grin.

Achilles squinted toward the Greek camp and the hammering. The fires lit up a monstrous wooden statue. "They're building a wooden cow!" he exclaimed.

"Shh!" the mouths hissed at him.

"No, boys. That's what the people on the walls of Troy are looking at. They can't see us in the moon shadows. They're looking at the pig!"

"The wooden swine of Troy," Paris said. "I wonder what that's all about."

"Never mind—it means you can drop those stones, Hec!" Achilles ordered.

"Aw! Do I *have* to?" Head 17 moaned.

"Just drop them anywhere."

"Seems a shame to waste them," Head 3 said. The monster wound back 50 pairs of arms and threw them at the walls. The Trojans screamed in panic as a storm of stones hit them, and the tops of the walls crumbled. They staggered home, bruised and bleeding, not sure what had happened out there in the darkness.

High above them, the Avenger settled next to Hera; she had already called Hermes, the messenger. The young man was complaining. "Dragged me out of my bed, you did! I didn't know I was supposed to be a twenty-four-hour delivery service! It's not fair. Nobody else has to come flying when you click your fingers. I'm going to complain to Zeus when I see him."

Hera sighed. "Hermes, just fetch three pairs of wings from Olympus and do it before dawn. Our friends must be off the plains before sunrise."

"Puh!" Hermes pouted and flew off with a buzz of feathers at his winged feet.

"Thank you," the Avenger said. "I will find Prometheus no matter how long it takes."

Hera smiled, and her teeth shone in the moonlight. "Oh, it won't take very long at all," she said.

"He could be anywhere. When that god dies, he gives off a green spark. I have to search Earth through time, looking for it."

"No, you don't," Hera said, teasing. "Not if someone told you exactly where to look and when."

The Avenger spread its wings, and its eyes burned so fiercely that they washed the dark streets of Troy with a red glow. "You know?"

Hera spread her hands. "Just go to Eden City. Eden City in the year the humans will call 1795."

"Yes-s-s-s!" The bird hissed so loudly that even the hammering horse builders stopped in wonder.

TEN

Now you may be worried that Theus would be grabbed by the Avenger and destroyed. Can you just stop worrying about him and think about ME for a change? I was going to be abandoned in this ugly city by my own pa, remember? Left as a hostage. Yes, we know that Pa said he had a plan to get us away, but Pa made a living from lying. Would YOU trust him?

Theus led the way to the Storm Inn. He seemed to know the city well, and the twisting lanes that confused me were no trouble to him.

"You've been here before?" I asked.

"Yes, in 1858," he said. "The city was even bigger then . . . I mean it *will be* even bigger then. Dirtier

111

and smokier," he said. "Just on this corner there'll be a factory owned by a Mr. Mucklethrift, and it'll vomit out purple smoke all day long till you choke on it even when you're a mile high."

I was sure then that I'd escaped from an old thief and fallen into the clutches of a young madman.

We passed the balloon that lay on the quayside as limp as a dead cat—yes, a red-and-white striped cat perhaps, but lifeless now that the hot breath of life had gone out.

Theus nodded. "Yes, I could carry that," he said.

I stopped suddenly. "I said I'd go out and look for a place to launch the balloon. We need quite a wide space without the buildings around. The quayside's just too narrow. We could fall into the water if we don't get it right."

Theus nodded. "Then we need to go to the prison."

"Huh?"

"There's an open space in front of the prison—about the only open space in Eden City," he explained. "It's big enough to hold five thousand people. They go there to watch."

"Watch what?"

"Prisoners being hanged," he explained.

"Nice."

"No, it's not nice at all. I was hanged there in 1858," he said.

"Crazy," I muttered. I reached into the basket of the balloon and pulled out some costumes. There was a red suit with white stripes that Pa used to wear sometimes. I found a black shirt and a black hat to go with it. "We need to dress you in these, or people will think you're a bit strange," I said.

"I know," Theus said. We waited for a cart to rattle past too fast and crossed the road to the Storm Inn.

There was a stage where singers and actors performed on Saturday nights. It was dark and quiet now. The red curtains were dusty and mottled. "Go behind there and change," I said. I went behind the bar and into the kitchen and found us a large meat pie to eat and a jug of ale to drink.

The kitchen table was as dirty as the barroom floor, but the pie was fresh. I left my 25 cents on the tabletop to pay for the food and carried it back to the barroom.

The suit was a little tight on Theus, but he looked good in it.

"I left my wings under the stage," he explained. "I may need them if the Avenger arrives suddenly."

I shook my head. "Look, Theus, we don't leave till this evening. Have some pie and ale and tell me your story."

That's what he did for the next couple of hours. I would repeat it now, but it would fill a book.[24]

Dusk came early to Eden City. Even without Mucklethrift factory, there was a dirty haze that hung over the city and blotted out everything but the midday sun.

Pa came down looking full of life after his long rest. He looked at Theus. "Perfect," he said. Theus described the square in front of the prison. "Perfect," Pa said. He peered at Theus in the gloom of the room. "I have a suit like that!" he said and laughed. "I use it for my fire-eating act."

"You eat fire?" Prometheus gasped. "I didn't give fire to the humans to eat," he mumbled.

That puzzled me, but Pa didn't seem to hear.

---

24 Theus reckoned that someone will be writing that book after 1858. So if you are reading THIS after 1858, there's a chance that you'll find that first book. He reckoned that it would be called *The Fire Thief* or something like that. But it's not my job to sell books for other writers! If you CAN'T find *The Fire Thief*, then just buy another copy of THIS book. I need the money.

"It's all a trick, my boy. I don't really eat it, you know. In fact, I could show you how I do it . . ."

"Pa!" I cut in. "We need to figure out how I'm going to escape from Eden City. The mayor and the sheriff want me to stay behind as a hostage."

Pa sat at the table, poured himself some of the ale, and sipped it. He made a face. "Cloudier than the Eden City sky and almost as sour as your ma!" he said.

"The plan!" I said.

"It's foolproof," he said. And he told us what it was. Theus was sent out to buy a net from one of the fishermen on the waterfront, and he stowed it in the balloon. I was given money to buy straw from the stables next to the inn and wool from the clothes shop on the corner. Theus went back out to buy a rope and rig it across the prison square.

It was completely dark by the time the owner of the Storm Inn came downstairs and opened the bar to the public. But people hadn't come to buy his bitter ale. They'd come to see the famous aeronaut— the man who was going to bring them guns and set them free (they thought).

The sheriff put a hand on my shoulder. "Stay close to me, little lady," he said.

"My name is Nell, not little lady," I said. "And I'm as tall as you are!" He looked surprised at my anger. I think he was worried that I might be more trouble than he had imagined. He jangled the handcuffs on his belt. My being chained up would ruin Pa's plan. I had to learn to control my temper.

There were crowds outside the inn, and they helped Theus carry the balloon and the basket to the prison square. Our wooden cannon was roped to the basket and trundled along behind.

The people of Eden City led the way, carrying lanterns that glowed yellow, as well as lights that were colored red and green, which they'd taken from the idle ships.

It was almost like a party procession. The pickpockets had the best of the party, of course, but no one could get near the bag of money that Mayor Makepeace carried with an armed guard.

Pa's plan meant that the crowd, the mayor, and the sheriff had to be distracted. He was going to give them a bit of a show so that they'd forget about little Nell, their hostage. Sadly, Pa forgot a few things too . . . but you'll soon find out what they were.

The balloon was placed in the square on the

cobbles, and the firebox was filled with the straw. Pa could have lit it with his tinderbox, but instead he took a long wax taper and lit that.

"And now," he roared above the noise of the jostling crowd. "Now I will light the flame that will heat the air and make the balloon rise."

There was polite clapping, and the crowd fell silent. They expected him to place the taper in the straw—instead he placed it to his mouth. He blew. A ball of fire shot out and lit hundreds of startled faces.

Theus turned to several of the children and said, "I gave that fire to humans, you know!" The children edged away from him and ran to cling onto their mothers' skirts. Can you blame them?

There were cheers. Pa did that a few more times before he blew his ball of flames into the firebox and set the straw on fire. I hurried across and piled the woolen material on top of the blazing straw. "My assistant, Nell, is making smoke," Pa declared. "It is the smoke that makes the balloon rise."[25]

25   YOU know that it is hot air that rises. YOU know that it isn't smoke that makes a hot-air balloon lift off the ground. But you have to remember that these were the first days of balloon flights. In those days, the aeronauts believed that it was smoke that let them fly. So, of course, Pa and I believed it too. It's in the history books if you don't believe me.

Theus stepped forward and held the balloon bag over the smoke, as Pa had told him to, so that the bag was filled. "It will take ten to fifteen minutes to fill," Pa told the crowd. "In the meantime, Miss Cobweb from England will perform on the tightrope!"

Four men were given the job of holding the fishnet under the rope in case I fell.

"Ooh!" the crowd cried as I climbed up a drainpipe on the side of a house and hoisted myself onto a rope that stretched across the square. I was supposed to slip once or twice to make the crowd gasp. (Really, they wanted me to fall—not because they hated me, but because it would be more exciting.)

But that night my slips were real enough. I was nervous about Pa's plan—and the wind was whipping over the water from East River City. For some reason, that upset me, but I didn't have the time to figure out why. Anyway, Pa should have figured it out for himself, but HE forgot. (And, by the way, YOU should have figured it out by now too!)

I staggered to the far side of the square and was glad to slide down the drainpipe to the solid, filthy cobbles. I ran to the balloon basket. It was filling quickly now and starting to strain on the ropes. "Hey!" Sheriff Spade called. "You aren't going to escape that easy. You stay here till Dr. Dee gets back with the guns!"

He grabbed my arm. "No," I hissed. "I'm just going to change into my Captain Dare costume," I told him. "I can't escape unless I'm in the basket at the same time as Dr. Dee and the money."

He nodded. "That'll never happen," he said grimly and let me climb in to change. The balloon above my head was tight now, and the ropes were straining. The next two minutes would bring us escape . . . or disaster.

I was changed and out of the basket in a minute. Pa was calling, ". . . and as I rise into the air, my friend Captain Dare will thrill you all by flying out of the cannon. I want you men with the net to stand by the prison wall. If Captain Dare misses, he will smash into the ground or be splattered against the prison wall!"

"Ooh," the crowd gasped. Half a minute to go. As I climbed into the mouth of the cannon, Pa climbed into the basket of the balloon. I looked toward the back of the cannon where Theus stood. "Best of luck, Theus," I said. "I hope you find your hero and escape from the Avenger."

"Thank you, Helen of Eden," he said with that handsome grin. "I will."

I let myself slip back into the darkness of the barrel.

As Pa shook hands with the mayor and took the cash bag, Theus stood with the lighted taper at the back of the cannon.

Fifteen seconds to go. "Untie the balloon!" Pa cried. It was tied to a metal ring attached to the prison wall—probably the place where they chained prisoners. Someone untied it, and the balloon jumped upward.

Theus took a rope that was fastened around the mouth of the cannon and wrapped it around his wrist. That would hold the cannon steady and give a better aim. A loose cannon could skid across the cobbles when it went off, and I could end up anywhere. I didn't want to end up anywhere. I was aiming for one place tonight . . . and it wasn't the net.

Five seconds.

"Freedom for Eden City!" Pa yelled, and the crowd cheered.

Theus pulled hard on the rope. From inside the barrel, I felt the cannon tip upward.

Two seconds. I looked out and didn't see the net—

I saw the balloon basket.

One second. Theus lit the fuse.

Whap! The spring sent me out of the barrel like a bullet, and I soared into the air. Pa stretched out his arms over the side of the balloon basket to catch me.

What a pity he forgot those two things!

ELEVEN

Sorry. I have to leave my story there with me hanging in the air between a balloon and a crowd that would tear me apart if I fell into their greedy clutches. Writers call that sort of ending a "cliff-hanger"—where our heroine is left hanging onto the edge of a cliff. Will she survive, you wonder? You have to read on, don't you, to find out. Very irritating. I wasn't even hanging onto a cliff edge—I was hanging onto the air between life and death. But we HAVE to get back to Greece.

Hermes was in a better mood when he arrived back in Troy with the wings for the hunters. He circled over the Greek camp, where the evening fires were dying down now. They were beads of light, strung

122

out like a glittering necklace. The sea beyond was midnight blue, the setting moon was as thin as a sickle, and the stars burned gold and green. The sky was turning the faintest shade of gray-pink in the east since dawn was close at hand.

It was a very peaceful scene in the middle of this tiresome war—only the endless hammering of the Greek carpenters shook the early morning air. But Hermes was content.

Even the monstrous 50-headed Hecatonchires down below him looked like a soft stuffed animal.

Hermes landed gently and placed the wings on the dusty earth in the shadow of the walls. "So what are you up to?" he asked the heroes.

The Avenger turned its savage beak on the messenger. "Mind your own business!"

Hermes' mouth fell open. His good mood vanished. "Well, there's gratitude for you. I'm dragged out of my bed to run errands for you, and that's the thanks I get."

The Avenger stepped toward the god with wings on his ankles and hissed, "When I have destroyed Prometheus, I may just come back and destroy you, Hermes, you idle, vain, and stupid little god."

"You can't do that! I haven't done anything wrong!" the god squeaked but didn't sound too sure.

"I'll think of something," the Avenger said in a breath as soft as the campfire flames and just as deadly. It turned away to collect the wings and pass them to its deadly new gang.

"Zeus would never let you! You're a big bully bird, that's what you are! I'm going to tell Zeus that you've been picking on me—threatening me. You'll be sorry."

The Avenger was as still as the Trojan walls. Then it turned very slowly back to Hermes.

"Oop!" Hermes gave a little hiccup of fear.

A long wing stretched out and wrapped itself around Hermes' shoulder. The messenger shivered. "Oop! Don't hurt me!"

Now the Avenger's voice was as soft as a spider's web. "Sorry, Hermes."

"What?"

"I shouldn't have threatened you. I am so glad you gave up your sleep to help me. There's no need to tell Zeus about my little outburst of temper, is there?"

"What? Oop!"

"We are on a secret mission to capture Prometheus, and we don't want our secret to get out. But I can trust you, can't I?"

"Yes. What? Oooop! Ahhhh!" Hermes had a sly look in his eyes. "You don't want Zeus to know what you're up to, do you?"

The Avenger tried to smile, but it's hard to smile when your mouth is a beak.[26] "It was Zeus who sent me to punish Prometheus," it said.

Hermes puffed out his lips, "Prrrr! But Zeus has changed his mind. He thinks that Theus has suffered enough. He would call you off if he could."

"He can't!"

"But he *could* if Theus performs a task. That's why he said Prometheus can go free if he finds a human hero."

Bony spurs on the Avenger's wing went tight around Hermes' shoulder. "Not if I get Theus first," it said.

Hermes wiggled and then stopped. His hiccups had disappeared. "Ooh!" he breathed. "*I* know what you're afraid of. Zeus ordered you to take Achilles and Paris to Hades. He doesn't know that you've set them free to help you. He certainly doesn't know that you've let that grotesque monster from hell loose too."

---

26 It's true, isn't it? When did you last see a greenfinch giggle, a sparrow snicker, a blue jay titter, or an albatross go tee-hee? Owls don't grin, and seagulls don't smirk because they can't. Sometimes it's a sad life being a bird.

"Here!" Head 35 of the Hecatonchires objected. "Watch who you're calling go-pest."

"Yeah," Head 17 said and nodded. "Our mom says we were gorgeous when we were a baby! What does 'go-pest' mean anyway?"

The Avenger pulled Hermes away from the others and said, "We fliers have to stick together, Hermes . . . friend."

"Friend? No one's ever called me that before. The other young gods are jealous of my wings, you know."

"Oh, I know. I have the same problem. So, when I get back, you and I will have to make sure that we're the best of friends. *Do* things together!"

"Things?"

"Go for a flight somewhere nice."

"Where?"

"The seaside."

"Great!" Hermes cried, happy again. "Can we build sand castles?"

"I'll call for you at Olympus as soon as I get back," the Avenger said.

"Promise?"

"Promise."

Hermes shook his head. "Funny, isn't it? Theus is

hunting a hero. You're hunting Theus, and Zeus would be hunting you if he knew about these three!"

"Sand castles," the Avenger said gently.

Hermes' ankle wings whirred, and he rose happily into the night air as the Avenger waved. When the messenger had gone beyond the clouds, the Avenger growled, "Birdbrain!"

It turned to its three helpers. "Get the wings strapped on. We need to be away from here before Zeus gets back from inside Troy. We've got a long journey ahead of us."

By the time the dawn sun blazed through the eastern hills, the color of blood, the Avenger, the two heroes, and the monster were flying toward it.

The bravest of the Trojan guards lifted their heads over the walls. One was as thin as a topless tower. The other was as fat as a barrel . . . which was odd in this starving city. "That rock thrower's gone. We're safe," the thin one said with a sigh.

"And that Greek statue looks finished. I told you it was a squirrel! The wooden squirrel of Troy," his fat friend said.

"It's a horse—the wooden horse of Troy," a voice said.

The guards turned and saw an old man with a white beard standing behind them. "How do you know, old man?"

"Call me Sinon," the shrunken figure said.

"How do you know, Simon?"

"Si-*non*!"

"Sorry, Si-*non*."

"I was a spy in the Greek camp. I heard them plan it. After Achilles died, they were very upset. Most of them said that they wanted to go home. Then *Paris* died, and the others agreed—they'd killed the man they'd come to kill," Sinon said.

"Makes sense," the tall, thin guard said.

"I *thought* they came to get Helen—they're not going to go back without the wife they came for," the barrel-bodied guard argued. "Not after ten years of trying."

"Ah," Sinon said. "They have their own wives back home in Greece. It's time to quit. Look!"

As the blood-red sun brightened to a fiery orange, the guards saw the tattered tents begin to come down.

More guards joined them on the wall that overlooked the sea. Then a trickle of Trojans climbed the walls to watch as word got around. "The Greeks are going!"

"Without Helen?"

"Looks like it. See? They're heading for the ships!"

"Aw! I'll miss them!"

"You *what*? Are you crazy? We're free."

"Suppose so."

By the time the sun was as white and hot as steel, it seemed like everyone in Troy was crowding onto the walls. "They've left without me," Helen said with a sigh. "I didn't think they'd ever leave without me."

King Priam shook his head. "Your face wouldn't launch four hundred ships these days."

"Thanks," Helen said bitterly. "No husband Menelaus, no boyfriend Paris, and hundreds of miles from home."

She watched as the sails of the Greek ships were raised and the fleet headed over the horizon. By afternoon, there wasn't a Greek to be seen.

"Open the gates of Troy!" King Priam ordered.

The order was echoed around the ancient city, "Open the gates of Troy!"

It rang around the city, voice to voice. Crier to crier.

Then the answer rang back. "Where are the keys? Where are the keys? Where are the keys?"

King Priam blushed. "Well, of course, I am the king and the keeper of the keys."

"So where are they, sire?"

"I . . . er . . . don't remember. It's been ten years since I last needed them. I can't remember where I put them. Sorry!"

Zeus (in the body of Sinon) looked toward the wooden horse and wondered how the Greek soldiers were managing without a bathroom inside. Something had to be done soon, or the whole plan would be ruined. He stepped forward. "Allow me, sire. In my youth I was an expert with locks."

"You were a locksmith?"

"No. A burglar. But I am sure that I can open the gates of Troy," he said.

"Give it a try, old man, and I'll be in your debt for life. I'll even let you marry Helen."

"No, thanks."

Zeus-Sinon walked down from the walls and looked at the lock. He blinked and looked again. He blinked again and looked again. He looked up to the king. "The gates aren't locked, sire," he called.

"What? We've kept the Greeks out for ten years, and nobody noticed that we'd forgotten to lock the gates? Oooops!" the king said with a laugh. "Better not put that in the history books, or we'll look like chuckleheads! Ah, well, open the gates of Troy!"

Sinon turned the handle, and the gates swung open for the first time in ten years. The wind from the plains swept in and blew away the stench of a dying city. It was like air rushing into a lung. It was like wine to the trapped people of Troy, and they drank in the sea-salt air.

Strangers hugged one another in the streets. Helen appeared from the palace to see what the fuss was all about. The crowds who had hated her gave her a cheer. A woman, drunk on the powerful air, jumped into the fountain in the weedy town square and called, "Three cheers for Helen of Sparta!"

"Nay, Helen of Troy!" someone shouted back.

"Helen of Troy she is! The face that launched three hundred ships! Hip! Hip . . ."

"It was a thousand," Helen said, but her protests were swallowed up in the wild cheers.

Sinon ran back up the stairs to the ramparts of the city walls. He ran too fast for an old man, but no one seemed to notice. "King Priam . . . you *must* get that wooden horse inside the city. Put it in the city square.

Let the people have a party with lots of wine."

"We will."

"But *soon*, sire. It's a big statue, and it will take all afternoon to move it. We have to have it in the city tonight," Sinon urged him.

"Why?"

"Because . . . it looks like rain!" Sinon said.

Priam squinted at the sky. There was only one cloud in sight. "It hasn't rained for weeks!"

Zeus waved up at the cloud and saw Hera listening. She nodded and waved her hands till she made a whirlwind that sucked up the sea into a cloud of slate gray that was ten times larger than Troy.

The shadow darkened the day. King Priam ran along the ramparts. "I want a hundred men to bring that horse inside. A hundred men, and I want them now! Hurry! We don't want our precious gift to get wet!"

Men and women ran out with ropes and fastened them around the legs of the wooden horse.

It was like a party game. They pulled and heaved till it started to roll. They marched faster and faster till some of them were trotting along. They began to sing in time to their steps. The horse jolted and creaked through the open gates and rolled to rest in the city square.

The people turned to Priam for praise. He looked down and ordered, "Turn off the water to the fountain!"

"What?" the thin guard gasped.

"And let the fountain flow with wine!"

"Wine? We haven't had wine for ten years," the fat guard said and sighed.

"Ah . . . yes . . . no . . . there may be a few hundred barrels in my palace cellars," Priam said and blushed.

"You miserable monarch," the fat guard cried. "You kept it all for yourself?"

"I didn't drink it," Priam said and pouted. "Well, not with *every* meal."

"Ha!" the fat guard growled and went off to help fill the fountain.

It was just like a party game. And every party game has to have a prize. The prize for capturing the Trojan horse was the greatest prize of all.

And its name was Death.[27]

27 Don't worry. As we leave Troy, I can tell you that not everyone died. That night the soldiers slipped from the bowels of the wooden horse and let in the Greeks who had sailed back. They only killed the men and boys—who would miss them? The girls and women were turned into slaves—which can be quite pleasant if you stay cheerful. And Helen? She was sent back to miserable Menelaus . . . which served her right. Her face would never launch another ship again.

TWELVE

*Remember where you left me? Fired from a cannon up into
the air. Shooting toward the waiting arms of my father. But
did he catch me? "He must have," you say. "Otherwise you
wouldn't be here telling us this story now," you say. If you
say that, then you are not quite as witless as you look. But
you have to remember that I wasn't safe yet—I did tell you
that there were TWO things that Pa forgot to do. Maybe
you haven't figured out what the two things were? I
suppose you want me to tell you? Oh, all right . . .*

As I sped up into the cool night air, I saw Pa's
grinning face ahead of me, and his large hands
grabbed me by the wrists.

134

A moment later he'd pulled me over the side and into the basket. "Ha!" he roared. "I *told* you to trust me! We have the money, *and* you're free."

I staggered to my feet and looked at the prison wall as we climbed past it. I tugged off my false mustache and looked back down.

The crowd was slow to take in what they'd seen. But Sheriff Spade wasn't. "My hostage! My hostage is getting away. I never lost a hostage in my life, and I'm not losing one now. Grab that man!"

Now, that sounded a little odd to me. What was the use telling people to grab Pa when Pa was sailing over their heads and out of their reach? And the other odd thing was that the sheriff wasn't really pointing at Pa. He was pointing at something below the basket.

I leaned over the side as far as I dared and looked under the basket. That's when I saw Pa's first "forgetting."

He'd forgotten to untie the cannon from the basket.[28] We reached the end of the rope and felt the

---

28 Yes, of course you spotted that, so you're sitting there as smug as a mouse in a cheese factory. You are saying, "Oh? Why didn't YOU remember, Nell?" Well, mouse face, I had a lot of other things to worry about—things like missing the balloon and ending up like a swatted fly on the jailhouse wall.

balloon's climb suddenly slow down. Pa looked over the side. Not only was the cannon hanging on the end, but Theus had the cannon rope wrapped around his wrist, and it was pulled tight. He was being lifted too.

With the cannon and Theus pulling us down, the balloon just didn't have enough smoke to sail into the clouds.

Sheriff Spade was one of the first to act. He jumped up to catch the dangling legs of Theus . . . but he was too short.

"Stop that man! I never lost a hostage yet, and I'm not gonna lose this one!"

The basket bumped against the prison wall and hung there. Pa and I were just about level with the top of the wall and could look down on the other side. Pale prisoners in gray rags looked up at us in wonder. Pa waved. "Just passing!" he called to them.

But if someone grabbed our god's legs, then we'd be "just passing" on the way back down.

"More wool on the burner, Nell," Pa ordered, and I climbed to the side of the basket to obey.

A few of the Eden City people tried to help the sheriff, but it's hard to look up and walk straight. A lot of them fell over one another into a pile on the cobbled square. A tall, thin man was our biggest danger. "Grab those legs, Mike Pike," the sheriff ordered. Mr. Pike looked up . . . and tripped up. He fell over an old lady's cane and knocked it away. She fell to the cobbles, and Mike Pike fell on top of her.

"That's my wife you're assaulting!" an old man cried and began to beat the thin man with his cane. Someone dragged the old man away, but a younger woman started to kick him. "Leave my ma alone, you bully!" she screamed. She kicked out but hit a boy in the backside. His mother slapped her face, and in moments 20 men and women were brawling, battling, and bruising each other underneath the basket. Only the sheriff kept his eyes on Theus and the dangling legs.

Then the sheriff had a great idea. "Go to the top of the prison wall and drag that couple out of the basket," he ordered.

"To the top of the prison wall!" the mayor roared over the top of the screams of the fighting people.

"To the top of the wall!" went the cry. Ten men rushed to the gate of the prison and collided with it.

"The gate's locked, Sheriff," one man shouted.

Sheriff Spade shook his fist wildly. "Locked? Locked? Locked? Why is the prison gate locked?"

"To keep the prisoners in, I guess," someone told him.

"Unlock the gate," the sheriff ordered.

"The prisoners will get away," someone cried, and a ripple of panic ran through the crowd.

"But if we don't get inside, my *hostage* will get away," the sheriff moaned and hammered on the door with his pistol.

Looking down on the hats and the upturned faces, I could see both sides of the prison gate. "Who's there?" a guard called from the inside.

The smoke from the balloon rose thickly, and the balloon edged up the wall with a grating sound. The sheriff looked up in panic. "It's the sheriff."

"How do I know?"

"Know what?"

"Know you're the sheriff," the guard said.

I waved at the guard. "It's NOT!" I called down. "It's a jail-breaking friend of Mad Dog McGrue!"

"Ooh! No! Help! We're being raided by Mad Dog McGrue's friends!" the guard wailed.

"No, you're not!" the sheriff cried.

"Yes, you are," I said as the balloon climbed an inch higher.

"You shut up!" the sheriff called to me.

"Help! Mad Dog McGrue's partner told me to shut up," the guard sobbed.

"I did NOT," the sheriff shouted.

"He did not," I agreed. I had to do some quick thinking. "He said, 'Shoot up.' He meant that he's going to shoot up the gate if you don't set Mad Dog McGrue free."

"No! No! No!" the guard said and waved his hands as if he was being attacked by a swarm of angry wasps. He looked up at me. "What can I DO?"

"Bring Mad Dog McGrue to the gate. Then if the man outside shoots at the gate, he'll shoot his friend!"

"Yes! Great idea. I will! I will! I will," the guard told me and ran inside the prison. The crowd outside had worn themselves out with fighting, and some staggered to lean on the prison wall, while some slumped to the ground.

Theus hung by his trapped wrist patiently. When you've spent 200 years chained to a rock, you must learn patience. When you've had your liver ripped out every day for those 200 years, an aching arm won't seem like much to suffer.

The sheriff squinted up at me and called, "If Mad Dog McGrue makes his escape, then he'll bring terror to Eden City. It will be all your fault."

The crowd turned their grubby and greasy faces toward me. "No, it won't," I said and laughed.

"Why not?" the mayor put in.

"Because there's no such person as Mad Dog McGrue. I just made him up."

"You did?"

"I did."

"Why?"

"To buy us some time while the smoke builds up," I told him.

The balloon swelled and inched up again. The mayor shook a fist angrily. "That is a VERY dangerous sort of man to invent, young lady. If you are going to invent make-believe friends, then invent a little puppy or a fairy—but NOT a crazy gunman who could scare the poor people of Eden City into nightmares!"

"Sorry," I said. The guard ran back to the gate. We were creeping clear of the top of the prison wall now, but someone could easily grab the cannon or Theus and haul us back.

The guard shouted through the gate. "The warden won't let Mad Dog McGrue out . . . but he says you can come in . . ."

"Then open the gate," the sheriff ordered.

"But you can only come in if you have a letter from the sheriff," the guard said.

"I AM the sheriff," the sheriff screamed.

"The warden said you have to prove it by giving me a letter from the sheriff," the guard went on.

I have heard of people tearing out their hair in a rage, but I'd never seen it till then as the sheriff threw his hat on the ground and grabbed his hair in both hands.[29]

"Give me some paper, someone," he begged the crowd. Someone ran off to find a piece while the cannon climbed above the wall. Only the legs of Theus could be caught now.

The sheriff scribbled a note with a quill, a paper bag, and an ink pot that a grocer brought him. We

---

29 This may hurt you, if you ever try it. But not as much as it hurt Sheriff Spade. He'd forgotten that he was holding a heavy pistol in his right hand when he threw his fists to his head. Crunch. Ouch.

were almost too high to catch now. The figures below were getting smaller, and I could hardly hear them.

"Here's the note from the sheriff," the sheriff said.

"I can't see it," the guard told him.

"Open the gate, and I'll show you."

"I can't do that. The prisoners will get away," the guard said. "You'll have to bring a note from the sheriff if you want me to open the gate and read your note from the sheriff."

The last I saw of the sheriff he was on his knees, sobbing and banging his head against the gate.

"Are you all right, Theus?" I called down.

"Don't worry about me," Theus said and gave a smile as if he made this sort of trip every day of his life.

I stoked up the grate with more straw, and the blaze made the balloon glow like a red-and-white striped moon. We were sailing on air—higher over the prison now. The twisted streets became like a tangle of dark wool, and the river ran its oily way to the west.

To the east, there was the blackness of the plains and the mountains. Small campfires of the Wild People twinkled, warm and welcoming.

That was when I realized that Pa had made a second mistake.

Of course someone as clever as you will have spotted that one too. So you don't need me to tell you what it was.

There may be one or two sad and simple readers who DON'T know what he'd done wrong. But I'm afraid that *they* will have to wait a little while to find out what clever readers like you already know . . .

THIRTEEN

SOMEWHERE OVER THE RAINBOW

It is almost the moment you have been waiting for. The time when my and Theus' story joins with the Avenger's. But not quite yet. Because Theus was hanging from our balloon. He wasn't where Hera had said he was . . . in Eden City. So the gruesome gang was close . . . but you don't get any prizes for being close.

The Avenger flew through space and time. The Hecatonchires flapped on behind. Sometimes the heads chatted to one another. Sometimes they chatted to Achilles and Paris.

"There are lots of moons out here," Head 7 said.

"I've heard that Earth's moon is made out of green cheese," Head 17 said.

"I like cheese," Head 41 put in. "Can we stop for a bite?"

"Yes, why not?" Head 37 agreed.

"Just going for a light lunch," Head 35 called to Achilles and Paris. "We'll catch up with you later!"

The Hecatonchires dived toward the green moon of the planet Soz and landed in a small village, and a family rushed out to see the stranger.

The man and wife, the young boy, and his older sister all had 50 heads and 100 arms.

The Hecatonchires waved 100 hands but soared on over the village to land in a field.

"They looked friendly enough," Head 17 said and grinned.

"Should we stop and say hello?" Head 11 asked.

Forty-nine heads turned as red as a sunset. "Too shy," they muttered.

The Hecatonchires picked up some Soz soil, and Head 22 tasted it. "What's it like?" Head 35 asked.

"Soil," Head 22 said with a sigh.

"Not cheese?"

"Not cheese."

"Better get on with the flight then," Head 43 said.

The godly wings flapped, and the Hecatonchires

lifted into the air. "It was a funny sort of planet," Head 47 told the others.

"Funny? The people looked just like us!" Head 35 argued. "Not like Earth, where those funny humans are missing forty-nine heads and ninety-eight arms!"

"Nah," Head 47 insisted. "Some people on this planet were ODD . . . they had long hair!"

"No! That was a girl."

"I've never met a girl before," Head 37 said with a sigh.

"She was pretty, wasn't she?" Head 16 said. Forty-nine heads agreed.

The Hecatonchires flew off into star-spotted space. That brief, cheese-seeking landing was soon forgotten by the Sozpeople.

But one Sozgirl smiled fondly as the Hecatonchires flew away. "He was handsome, wasn't he?" Head 16 said. Forty-nine heads agreed.

The Hecatonchires joined the others. When the Avenger's gang reached the farthest star, they turned right—because that was the way to move forward in time. The Avenger swung around and led them back to Earth the way that a goose leads its flock in a "V" shape.

Earth appeared, and the group swept to the dark side, where Eden City smoldered like a piece of rotting seaweed on a hot night.

Paris wrinkled his fine nose as they dropped to the top of the purple clouds. "It smells worse than the Hecatonchires!" he said with a sniff.

Achilles flew alongside him. "You have the stomach of a sickly kitten," he sneered.

"No! I swear that I've smelled that somewhere before. In the temple. When the priests make a sacrifice to Zeus."

Achilles shrugged. "Burning lamb?"

"No. Sometimes the priests get lazy and just throw the whole sheep on the sacrifice fire," Paris said.

"Burning wool? You can smell burning wool?"

"Yes!" Paris said, excited. "Maybe there's a temple here where the lazy priests are making a sacrifice to Zeus . . . look out!"

He added the last two words because suddenly a huge red-and-white striped ball loomed up out of the cloud ahead of them. It had some strange writing on the side that the heroes didn't understand . . . even if they'd had time to read it. The Avenger swooped easily around the side of the monster ball while the

Hecatonchires bobbed up, and 50 heads screamed, "Wheeee!" at the same time.

Two humans were sitting in a basket below the ball, but they were too dazzled by the flames from the burning straw and wool to see the four fantastic fliers in the midnight sky.

A rope dangled over the edge of the basket, and something was weighing down the rope. But whatever was there was hidden in the thick clouds.

The Avenger dived down toward Eden City and slowed. People were trudging wearily along the streets and seemed to be making their way home. One or two carried flares made from twisted twigs, and the flames reflected in the eyes of the robbers who hid in the alleyways. Some of the men carried muskets and headed for the city walls.

The Avenger signaled for its three helpers to stay in the air till all was quiet.

When the last light dimmed in the last house and the city settled into oily darkness, the Avenger led them down to the waterfront. Paris and Achilles landed softly on the quayside beside the hunched shadow of the Avenger. The Hecatonchires managed to clumsily snap off the mast of a ship that was already broken. It scattered empty lobster pots across the quay and then tangled its two legs in a pile of fishnets. "Oooops," Heads 21, 36, and 43 cried together.

A frightened dog barked at them and then scampered away into an alley at the side of the Storm Inn to hide and try to forget the nightmare that it had just seen.

The Avenger ordered the Hecatonchires to hide below the deck of the abandoned ship with the broken mast. It passed the wings of the heroes down into the ship's hold and ordered the monster to guard them. Achilles and Paris fell asleep on the coarse pile of nets and left the Avenger alone with its thoughts. They were dark thoughts. Thoughts of chains and rocks. Thoughts of revenge and raw liver. It crossed the road to the Storm Inn. The place was asleep. The snoring of 20 travelers shook the shutters. The birdlike beast couldn't sense that a Titan god had been inside. Maybe tomorrow morning it would go in and ask some questions. If Theus was back in Eden City, then the Storm Inn would be the place that he'd go.

The Storm Inn . . . or the Temple of the Hero. The bird shuffled along the deserted streets, trying to remember the way to the temple. It plodded past a house with a sign saying, "Mrs Waters' Wonderful world for Children. The Nicest Nursery in Town."

Babies coughed and mewled weakly behind the cob-webbed windows. The Avenger paused a moment and looked in to see a round-shouldered old woman lit by a weak and smoky candle. "I'm busy, Mrs. Waters. So very busy. But one day I may be back for you to take you straight to Hades. One day."

The old woman looked up from the cradle where she sat with a stump of a candle and spooned food into the mouth of a dark-haired baby. She shivered and warmed her hands at the candle. "Brrrr! I think someone just walked over my grave," she cackled.

It was truer than she thought.

The Avenger shuffled on, its claws scratching along the wooden sidewalks. A faded sign said, "To the Temple of the Hero."

The street was a dark shadow. The lane that led to the temple was a shadow of a shadow—darker than the underworld of Hades. The Avenger stepped into the inky air.

There was a soft swish in the air, and a blade brushed against its feathered throat. "Your money or your life?" an old man's voice creaked in the coal-cellar blackness.

"My life," the Avenger whispered.

"Eh? You're not supposed to say that."

"So sorry to disappoint you," the Avenger breathed. With a swift move of its head, it had the blade in its beak. A moment later a crunch of the beak shattered the steel blade.

"That cost me fifty cents!" the old man complained. He wore a very dirty handkerchief over the bottom half of his face. He lifted it angrily. "I'll report you to Sheriff Spade, I will! I need that knife to make my living. That's a tool of my trade, that is. I'm the Phantom of the Night . . ."

"The what?"

"Phantom of the Night. I'm famous in Eden City, I am. The Masked Marauder, they call me."

"I thought they called you the Phantom of the Night?"

"At night they do. In the daytime they call me the Masked Marauder. Anyway, I could have the law on you! You owe me sixty cents."

"I thought you said it cost you fifty cents."

"The price has gone up since I bought that knife.

In fact, you can't *get* them anymore. You've ruined my life," the old man said, and his pale eyes glowed in the dark street.

The Avenger had met many angry people but had never met this problem before. "I'm . . . sorry," it stammered. Then it snapped its beak shut and shook its feathered head. "No, I'm not. You tried to *rob* me! You're a *thief*!"

"Even a thief has his rights," the old man said. "I have a right to be paid for the damage you did to my knife."

"No, you *don't*!"

"Then let's see what Sheriff Spade has to say, shall we?"

The Avenger was foaming at the beak with rage. "Listen carefully. I am going to kill you and take your spirit straight to Hades if you don't do as I say."

"No need to be like that," the old man huffed.

"I AM like that. It's MY job to be like that. So close your toothless mouth and listen . . ."

"Ha! You're a fine one to talk about being toothless," the man grumbled.

The Avenger ignored him. "Listen, Mr. Waters. I will spare your life if you can help me."

"How do you know my real name? I am the Phantom of the Night!"

"I know more than you think," the beak hissed. "The one thing I do not know is where my prey is."

"If you want to pray, you can go to the temple . . ."

"Prey, I said. The man I am seeking—his name is Prometheus."

"Never heard of him."

"No, but you may have *seen* him. He is tall compared to you miserable humans. He has long, dark hair and golden skin. You would probably call him handsome. He has white wings and flies."

"He has flies? So does the garbage dump at the end of our street," the old man said.

The Avenger gave a grating sigh. "I *mean* he has the power of flight."

"Ah! You mean Dr. Dee!"

"Do I?"

"A showman in a top hat. He flies. He has a young daughter who walks on ropes."

"No, no, that doesn't sound like him. Prometheus would look like a young man to you."

"Well, you could be talking about Dr. Dee's assistant. He wears a red-and-white striped suit.

Very strong."

"That sounds like him," the Avenger said, and his claws clacked on the cobbles as he shifted his feet, excited. "Where can I find him?"

"Oh, he escaped earlier tonight. Got caught in the balloon and flew off."

"Balloon?"

"Big bag of hot air. They have a sack full of money that they tricked the people of Eden City out of. I hate them."

"Because they tricked you?"

"No, because it's such a great idea. I wish I'd thought of it," Mr. Waters, the Phantom of the Night, said with a sigh. "I'd be rich now. I wouldn't have to wander the streets phantoming people, would I? I mean, it's bad for my old feet is this marauding all day and then phantoming all night. It's a killer!"

"So am I, Mr. Waters," the bird breathed. "But you have been useful to me, so I am going to let you go free."

"What about my knife?"

The bird blinked and leaned toward the old man. Its sour breath made his watery eyes stream. "Knife?

I am giving you your *life*. Now, tell me, where did they fly to in this baboon?"

"Balloon."

"Baboon, balloon . . . who cares? Just tell me where they were headed."

"That's the strange thing!" The old man gasped and wiped his nose on the handkerchief around his face. "They flew off to the west . . . they headed for the country of the Wild People! They'll lose their scalps! They're as good as dead!"

FOURTEEN

THE PLAINS OF EDEN CITY—1795

It sends a chill through your body, doesn't it? Imagine going to a hairdresser for a haircut. He slips a stone knife underneath the front of your hair and pulls backward. Whoosh! You'll never need a haircut again! I wonder what would happen to a bald man? Would they scalp him anyway and use the scalp to patch the elbows in their shirts? It was one thing I never got to ask the Wild People. Anyway, they weren't the scalping savages we imagined, which was just as well . . .

You'll have spotted Pa's second "forgetting" before I did. I was just so *pleased* to have escaped from Eden City that I didn't think of where we were going. We climbed through a cloud, and three or four gigantic birds rushed past us and made the balloon shake.

Pa fell to one side and grabbed a rope. It was just bad luck that he grabbed the rope that let the hot air out of the balloon. There was a hiss, and we dropped sharply back into the cloud. "More straw and wool on the burner, Nell!" Pa told me.

"We've got none left," I told him. "We had just enough to get across the river, but we've already used too much getting free of the prison wall," I said. "Looks like we'll land in the river and drown after all."

I looked over the side to see if Theus was still with us. He'd be all right. He could swim and maybe drown, but he could come back to life— swim and drown and come back to life as many times as he liked until he reached safety. I couldn't.

"Are you still there, Theus? Those birds have lost us a lot of smoke. We're going down."

"They weren't birds," he called up. "That was the Avenger—the one that's hunting me. It has the help of Achilles and Paris, and it looked like a Hecatonchires, too."[30]

---

30 I know what you think: if Theus saw them, then why didn't they see him? Well, if you are in a mist, then it hides you from someone outside the mist. But often you can look out and see people outside. Oh, I know what I mean. Anyway, Theus came out of the cloud when they had passed, and he saw their backs quite clearly.

We dropped through the underside of the cloud. Theus waved his free hand, and I looked for the oily waters of the river, waiting to suck us under to a clammy death. Instead I saw bright fires in the center of a circle of tents, and I knew that Pa had had a second "forgetting." "Pa!" I cried. "Did you remember to check the wind? Was it blowing from the east or the west before we left Eden City?"

He shrugged. "They said that it blows from the west in the evenings."

"Well, they were wrong. We aren't heading to East River City—we're heading over the plains to the camps of the Wild People!"

"That's never happened to me in all my years as a balloonist," he said.

"All your years? Yesterday was the first time you've ever flown free . . ."

"The Montgolfier brothers in Paris . . ."

"No, Pa!" I yelled at him. "That was just a story you made up to fool the suckers, remember? You're not really a balloonist . . . you're a showman."

"I guess you're right, Nell," he said sadly.

"And you're soon going to be a scalped showman," I moaned.

We dropped steadily toward the circle of tents, and warriors in suits made out of animal skin came out to watch us. They mostly carried stone-headed hatchets and bows and arrows. I guessed it would be the hatchets they would use to scalp us.

It would hurt. I hoped that the landing would kill us first.

But the landing was as gentle as a feather on a sheet of silk. I had forgotten that Theus was a flier. He landed first. He placed the cannon on the soft grass—prairie grass that had been cropped short by the Wild People's ponies—and then he reached up and held the basket in his powerful arms.

He lowered us onto the grass. Pa snatched his hat and jammed it on top of his head.

"That won't stop them from scalping you," I said.

"It's not supposed to!" he replied. "If we are going to go, then let's give them a show!"

"What?"

"Let's do what we did when we landed in Eden City and put on a show for the Wild People. They probably haven't seen anything like us before. These simple folk may even think that we're gods who've come down from the sky!"

"Huh?"

Pa was usually right. I hurried to dress as Miss Cobweb and looked for somewhere to string a tightrope. The Wild People's tents were pointed at the top—a rope could go from tent top to tent top, I thought.

I whispered a quick order to Theus because he was tall enough to reach the tent tops without ladders. He took the rope from the cannon and set to work. Pa figured out what we were doing and started his show.

"Welcome to Dr. Dee's most amazing Carnival of Danger!" he said and smiled at the puzzled warriors. "This evening you will see my talented team of plucky performers daring to defy death. In fact, my friends, I have to warn you that some of them may *not* survive the dangers. Some days, Death wins. If you are upset by the sight of mangled bodies and bleeding corpses, then please go home now . . ."

No one moved. No one smiled. He turned to the basket and coughed. "Miss Cobweb . . ." he said loudly and paused. He looked toward the basket with a frown. ". . . will not just walk on the wire, she will *dance* on the wire!" He dropped his voice. "Are you ready yet, Nell?"

"I can't find the frilly pants for Miss Cobweb!" I squeaked back.

"Go on without them!"

"What!" I squawked. "Dance on the rope with no pants? No, thanks!"

"Would you rather lose your scalp?"

"Well, Pa, yes, I *would* if I have to choose!" I dived back in the basket and rooted in the clothes box.

Pa turned back to the ring of warriors. "While we wait, I will show you my fabulous fire-eating act!" he told them. He took a small bottle of alcohol from his coat pocket and sipped some. Then he marched to the log fire and pulled a long stick from it. He blew out a big globe of flames like a ball of fire.

Audiences normally screamed at this, and children hid behind their mothers' skirts. The Wild People stayed silent. I found the pants and pulled them on.

Pa tried every fire trick he knew, but the Wild People kept their faces as stony as their ax heads. Pa finished by spitting three fireballs into the air—one after the other—and lit the night sky. It was a sensation. He swept off his top hat and took a bow.

The warriors shook their heads and looked at a boy around my age. He wore pants made out of animal skin but no shirt. He stepped forward and took the flaming stick from Pa.

The boy placed the burning end against his bare arm and ran it up and down, and then he ran it across his chest. My mouth fell open with horror, but the boy showed no pain and no burns. He turned and used the stick to scatter some of the fire's glowing ashes over the ground. Then he stepped onto the ashes and walked slowly across them.

The boy stepped in front of Pa and took a bow. The warriors cheered and laughed. Pa clapped politely with a wide but worried grin.

"Now, famous Miss Cobweb from England—in her famous frilly pants—will dance on the rope! Give her a warm round of applause!" he said and clapped wildly. No one joined in.

Theus lifted me onto the rope. I had to walk and dance with no net below me. It was high enough to break a few bones, and some of my wobbles were real. I finished with a spin, a bow, and jumped into Theus' waiting arms.

The boy ran up the sloping side of the tent with no help. He jumped onto the rope, but he didn't walk across it or dance across it. He did tumbles and cartwheels across it. He swung from it, balanced on it, and leaped across it. He dropped off it, caught it with one arm, and let himself drop to the ground. This time he walked over to me and bowed as his friends cheered.

I felt my face turning redder than our balloon's red stripes. He'd made me look like the biggest fool ever to step off a balloon. That's when Theus, the hero, stepped forward and stopped my blushes.

He walked up to the smirking boy and took the hatchet from his belt. Then he placed his hand on a rock and brought the sharp edge down suddenly. Theus' finger flew off and into the fire.

The boy looked stunned. I thought that Pa was going to faint. I was the only one who knew that Theus would grow a new liver before the day had passed—I guessed he could also grow a new finger.

Theus passed the hatchet back to the boy and tilted his head as if to say, "Your turn."

The boy shook his head slowly. "You win," he said. Then he turned to me and Pa and said, "I knew you Wild Folk were crazy, but I didn't know you were *that* crazy."

"You speak English?" I asked.

He shrugged. "We tried to trade with the Wild Folk behind the wooden walls. We learned."

"We're not Wild Folk," I said.

"You come from the place that they call Eden City, don't you?"

"Yes."

"We call you the Wild Folk," he said.

"They call you the Wild People!" I told him.

He nodded. "They would."

"You're not wild? You don't scalp people?" I asked.

He gave a small smile. "Never. It's a story they put out to make the Wild Folk . . . I mean the people of Eden City . . . to make them fear us and kill us when they have the chance."

"We're not really from Eden City," Pa told the boy. "We're travelers. We belong nowhere."

The boy's smile was wide and bright now. "So are we. My people roam the plains hunting and fishing. We have no towns like Eden City."

"*Your* people?" Theus asked. "You are a chief?"

The boy nodded. "I am called Running Bear."

"Because you run round with no clothes on?" I asked.

The boy threw up his eyes. "Bear . . . the big, furry

animal. I don't run around *bare* naked."

"Sorry," I muttered.

"My father was the bravest of the brave," he said. "But the Wild Folk of Eden City have special weapons that they call guns. They use fire and spit out metal bullets. The guns killed him. Even my father couldn't face the Eden City bullets and live."

"Sorry," Theus said.

"Sorry?"

"For giving them fire. I stole it and gave it to the humans. I had no idea . . ." he began. He looked at his feet, suddenly ashamed.

"They will use their metal guns to destroy us in time," the boy said.

"Is that why you're attacking Eden City now?" Pa asked. "Trying to kill them before they kill you?"

Running Bear frowned. "No. If we kill all Eden City Wild Folk, they will only send more from over the river. We don't want to kill any of them."

I was puzzled. "You are surrounding the city. They can't get food in, and they can't get out. It's a siege."

"Like Troy," Theus put in.

Running Bear spread his hands. "The mayor said his name was Making Peace . . ."

"Mayor Makepeace?"

"He told us that the people of his city wanted to take our plains and turn them into farms. He said he would give us guns and gold, and we could move across the mountains."

"And you don't want to go. That's why you are attacking?" Pa asked.

"No, that is not why. The Mayor of Making Peace said he wanted to talk peace in our camp. He came with his lawmakers and his guns. We talked just a short while. He could see that we were never going to give up our land, and he smiled and said he would make us an even richer offer the next day."

"More gold?" Pa asked. Pa liked gold.

"What use is gold to us? No, while the mayor talked of peace, his lawman, with the hair on his face, waited outside . . ."

"Sheriff Spade?" I said.

"Yes. His sheriff. That man stole my baby sister, Prairie Rose, from her tent and carried her back to Eden City. That night he made us his offer . . . give up our land and we can have our princess back."

Theus closed his eyes and murmured, "They are holding a princess prisoner in Eden City just as the

Trojans held Helen of Sparta."

"My father led a party to rescue her, but we cannot climb their walls while they have guns and we have bows," he said, and there was pain in his eyes. "They killed him."

"So you have to starve them till they surrender?" I asked.

"Or give up the land. That is our only choice."

There was silence except for a soft wind blowing the campfire into crackling sparks.

"It's not your only choice," Theus said.

We all looked at him. "What else can we do?"[31] I asked.

"We can rescue her," Theus said simply. "Rescue their princess from her Troy."

---

31 I remember saying "we." I don't remember when I decided we were suddenly on the side of the Wild People of the plains. But Pa and Theus didn't argue. They must have decided around the same time that we were fighting against Eden City.

FIFTEEN

TROY—4,000 YEARS AGO—AND EDEN CITY, 1795

Those old Greek gods were snobs. They hated the pathetic little humans. But they couldn't stop meddling in human affairs. Even when the siege of Troy was over, they still wanted more fun. Maybe another siege to play games with . . .

Hera and Zeus looked down on Troy from their cloud. It was a sad sight.

The palaces and towers were smoking ruins with black and burned timber sticking out from charred walls, like ribs from a dead dog that some birds had torn apart.

Crimson wine flowed through the streets from the fountain and mingled with the cherry-red blood of the men and boys.

Everyone seemed to be moving so slowly. The Trojan women slaves were roped together and driven out over the plains to the waiting boats. Greek soldiers dug wearily on the plains to make deep pits and throw in their victims. They dragged them by the legs and let them slide down into the dusty graves.

Other soldiers sweated with huge tree trunks to lever the stones of the old walls and send them tumbling to ruin. From time to time a voice was raised in anger.

"Oy! Watch where you're tumbling that wall . . . you almost hit me with that topless tower."

"You should watch where you're standing, pal!"

"I was *told* to dig this grave here. It's more than my job's worth to move. So be more careful, or I'll come in there and shove this spade in your big mouth."

"I'd like to see you try!"

"Oh, yeah? You want a fight, do you?"

There was a silence as hundreds of soldiers listened and waited. Then, "No . . . I've been fighting for ten years. Enough's enough. Sorry, pal."

"All right, pal."

And the shoveling, slave shifting, and tumbling went on for a few more days. The Greeks left, and the rats returned. The windy plains drifted their sand over the ruins and turned Troy into a memory.

"I'm bored now," Hera said.

Zeus looked at her. "You were bored because the siege went on and on. I did something about it. Now you're bored again because the siege is over. You are *never* satisfied, are you?"

The goddess shrugged. "Couldn't you find us another, more exciting siege? One that lasts ten weeks, not ten years?"

Zeus sighed. "As it happens, Cousin Theus is at one right now. Mind you, it's four thousand years into the future."

"Take me there," Hera ordered. "Does it have a hostage princess? And heroes? And villains? Take me there."

"Oh, all right," Zeus said with a sigh and used his godly powers to move the cloud from the windy plains of Troy to the windy plains of Eden City.[32]

---

32 The ordinary gods had to fly through space to move through time, of course. But Zeus was no ordinary god. He was the chief god, and he could move through time and space with a special power that no one else had. It was a power he rarely used—so he's not likely to pop up and look over your shoulder as you read this. The truth is that he was too lazy to enjoy this wonderful gift. He had to be nagged by someone like Hera. I am nagged by my landlord to pay the rent, so I write this book. We all need a little push from time to time, don't we?

As the cloud moved around to the other side of Earth, the Sun (which makes time) began to spin through the sky faster and faster till it was a blur.

There are 365 days in one year, and Earth spun through almost 4,000 years. Four thousand times 365. That's . . . a lot.

The spinning slowed, and Zeus' cloud arrived above the plains of Eden City. Zeus and Hera studied the people. "This time *I* want to join in. I can't spend my life sitting here just watching the little human theater. I want to be on the stage, acting. Tell me what to do."

Zeus was pleased to let Hera take over. It would give him a rest . . . I *told* you he was lazy. So he explained to her about disguising herself, and he told her about the plot to break the city defenses. Then she lowered herself to Earth and arrived in the middle of Running Bear's camp at sunrise. It was the morning after we'd arrived in the middle of the night. Everyone was sleepy. That's when I first saw her. We were heating some cornmeal into a porridge for breakfast when she walked into the circle of tents.

She looked like a warrior queen in bronze armor

and was carrying a shield and spear. The Wild People looked at her as if she was a being from another planet. "Greetings, simple human creatures," she said.

Running Bear jumped to his feet and faced her. Hera had gotten her size a little wrong, and she was too tall for a human woman. Running Bear and I came up to her belt buckle. "We are not simple," the boy told her.

"And we're not creatures," I added.

She ignored us. "I have come among you to rescue your princess from the evil city!" she said, as if she was an actress on the stage or Pa trying to attract a crowd.

"We already have a plan," I told her.

It was almost as if she was deaf.

"I have made a fine wooden statue of a horse!" she said and pointed through a gap between the tents to where a carved horse stood on wheels. It was as high as the walls of Eden City and very lifelike. "Your soldiers can enter the city inside the horse and massacre their men and boys as they sleep."

"We don't want to massacre anyone," Theus said. "We have a plan just to rescue the princess . . ."

She looked at him. "Oh, it's you, Theus. Trust you

to try to protect your precious little humans. You can't make a sacrifice without killing goats, we always say. You can't rescue a princess without a good old massacre. Look at Troy."

"I have a plan . . ." Theus began.

"A plan? Ha! Simple plans are always the best. I will go into the city, inside the horse, and open the gates at night. You bring your army in to kill the men and boys. Simple."

"There's no need for anyone to die," Theus started to argue, but Hera had closed her ears again.

"Blood will flow in the streets!" the goddess cried. "The princess will be returned to her happy husband . . ."

"She doesn't have a husband . . . she's not even one year old," Running Bear tried to explain.

"The city shall be burned to the ground!" she cried. Then she looked around at the warriors, who were spooning porridge into their mouths from their wooden bowls. "Who will join me inside the horse and bring glory to the tribe?"

The warriors looked at each other. One spoke up. "Has it got a bathroom inside?" he asked.

"Of course not!" Hera told him.

"Then you won't get me up in that!" he said, and the others nodded.

"Then I shall go alone. All the great heroes of the world must fight alone. The glory shall be mine, all mine!" she cried. "I'll just get inside, and you can pull it to the gates of the city," she added.

We rose wearily. "Where did *she* come from?" I muttered to Theus.

He sighed. "Sorry," he told me. "That's my cousin Hera in disguise. The wife of Cousin Zeus."

He looked up at a lonely cloud in the morning sky over the camp. He saw something that I couldn't see. He waved and then smiled. "Yes, Zeus is here."

I squinted at the bright cloud but saw nothing but a golden glow that could have been the morning sun reflected. "What do we do?"

"Let her try, I suppose. We have nothing to lose. The main thing is that the baby Prairie Rose is rescued."

"What if she kills everyone in Eden City?" I asked.

"They have Achilles and Paris to defend them," Theus said. "But she may get through the gates, and we can slip in behind her."

As the wooden horse was dragged over the plains,

Theus told Running Bear about our plan. "Nell and I will go into the city when they open the gates and bring out the princess."

"I'll come with you," the boy said.

"No," Theus told him. "You look like one of the Wild People. They will kill you as soon as they see you inside the city."

Running Bear grumbled and argued but had to give way in the end. We walked behind the wooden horse, and it came to rest around 50 paces from the gates of Eden City. Theus and I lay in the long grass and waited.

As the morning passed, the Wild People's tents were taken down, and the warriors moved back to the foothills of the mountains, out of sight. The people of Eden City came to the walls to look at the strange horse.

In the afternoon the gates swung open, and we heard footsteps in the long grass. "Well, well, well! A wooden horse!" Mayor Makepeace said.

The voice of the sheriff laughed. "That old trick from the story of Troy, eh?"

Theus moved sharply and whispered, "Even after all this time, you humans remember the story of Troy?"

"Of course! I would have told your Hera that, but she didn't seem to be listening," I said.

"So the horse trick won't work a second time?"

"Not even Mayor Makepeace is *that* stupid," I said.

Sure enough, the mayor said, "Grab some dried grass and pile it up underneath the horse. If it's wood, it'll burn."

There was a rustling as the sheriff and his helpers gathered grass. Then there was a crackling when they set fire to it.

"Should we go and look at that balloon out there on the plains? See if that robbing, cheating, lying Dr. Dee's around?" the mayor asked.

"No, the Wild People will have him by now. He'll be scalped and most likely eaten," I heard the sheriff say.

"Lucky man."

"Lucky?"

"Yep. Lucky. Because scalped and eaten is *nothing* compared to what the people of Eden City would have done if they'd gotten their hands on him."

"True," the sheriff said and chuckled. "Now stand back, Mayor. The wooden horse is ablaze. Let the Wild People inside roast. We'd better get back to the city and watch in comfort."

Even in the shelter of the grass, we could hear the roar of the fire.

We looked up and saw the flames wrap themselves around the body of the horse. There was a hideous scream. "This isn't how it's supposed to go!" Hera cried. "I'm burning!"

The heat and the smoke drifted over to our hiding place. We raised our heads just enough to see the party from Eden City walk back through the walls laughing. The gates slammed behind them.

The horse burned fiercely, and then the legs began to crumble to ashes, and the body crumpled to the ground before it fell apart in a shower of sparks.

Hera stood in the glowing ashes of the wooden horse. Her shining armor was soot, her hair was black dust under her helmet, and her shield was a smoldering, twisted ruin. "Zeus!" she cried to the sky. "I want to go home! Take me away from these *dreadful* people at once! If that simple tribe wants their princess back, then Theus can just get on with it."

I heard the gasps from the watchers on the Eden City walls as Hera rose up toward the cloud, and the cloud sped over the mountains and disappeared.

The wind on the plains blew the ashes into a swirling cloud, and the grass swished and swayed. Then Theus gripped my arm and held it tight. He pointed toward the city and then used that same finger to press against his lips. His godly ears could hear something. As they came closer, I could hear the footsteps for myself. They stopped, and a creaking voice spoke—a voice so cruel that it chilled me to my toes and froze me up to my hair.

"So, Achilles, our friend Theus has got a plan to enter the city and rescue this princess, has he?"

"Yes, Avenger, that's what it sounded like to me," a young man replied.

"Then we'll be waiting for him," the evil voice cackled.

"We don't know *how* he'll try to get inside Eden City, Avenger. It's guarded better than Troy. You Greeks took ten years to get in there," another young man put in.

"But we got you in the end, Paris," the first young man said.

"Only with that stupid horse trick . . ."

"Stop arguing," the Avenger hissed. "The Greeks

didn't have one of those balloon things. Theus does. Look. Now that the tents are gone, you can see it lying out on the plains."

"So?" Achilles asked.

"So, when it gets dark, Theus will fly the balloon over the walls of the city and rescue the princess," the Avenger said.

"How do you know?" Paris asked.

"Because that's what I'd do if I was Theus. But he doesn't know that I'll be waiting for him, and I will destroy him forever!"

"No, no!" Paris argued. "The Greeks got away with it because they *hid* their raiders inside the horse. Theus can't hide the balloon. As soon as the Eden City guards see the balloon, they'll shoot at him with their guns."

The Avenger seemed to stamp its foot. "Then Theus needs some help. He needs something to get the guards off the walls. Something to make them keep their heads down while he flies over."

"Something like the Hecatonchires?" Paris asked.

"Exactly," the Avenger hissed. "We send our friend Hec to help Theus. But we know that he'll be helping Theus land in my waiting claws!"

"Sounds like a good plan," Achilles agreed.

"So go and get Hec from his hiding place in the ship. Fly him over to the plains and tell him to wait beside the balloon. Tell him to help Theus."

"Do you think Theus will use Hec to help? It's a risk," Paris asked.

"I know Theus, and I know his weakness—he will take risks . . . and he's stupid enough to fall for it. No one escapes the Avenger for long. Prometheus must be destroyed. Tonight is his last night on Earth. Ever!"

SIXTEEN

Sometimes it's hard to be a writer. So many things were happening in Eden City and around it that it's hard to remember which order they happened in. Try to follow . . .

When the wooden horse of Eden City went up in flames, the Wild People warriors came back from the hills and set up their camps on the plains again.

Theus and I sat gloomily by the balloon while Pa worked to patch it up. "If the Avenger is waiting for me, I'll never get to the Temple of the Hero inside the city. I'll never find out who that human hero was and win my freedom."

"And Pa and I will never be able to fly back to East River City and spend the loot he stole from

Eden City," I said.

"And Running Bear will never set his sister free."[33]

As the sun fell in an orange ball below the mountains, Running Bear called a council of war.

All we seemed to talk about was what we COULDN'T do.

. . . we *couldn't* climb the walls because the defenders had guns, and they'd shoot us all . . .

. . . we *couldn't* fly over the walls in the balloon—even if the wind changed, the guards would shoot us down . . .

. . . we *couldn't* fire Theus over the walls in the cannon—he'd be killed and could come back to life, but the Avenger would find him and destroy him before Prairie Rose was rescued . . .

. . . we *couldn't* march up to the gates and ask to get in because the people of Eden City were after Pa and wanted their money back . . .

. . . we *couldn't* send Theus or Pa or Running Bear into the city at all . . .

33 Everyone likes a good moan at times. But that evening we had more moans than a porcupine has quills. If moans were bones, we'd have filled a graveyard. We were down, defeated, and desperate. Next time YOU feel like moaning, just remember how miserable WE were. You could NEVER get as moanful as we were.

. . . we *couldn't* send me in because, even if I rescued the Wild People's princess, I couldn't get her out.

Theus said, "The Hecatonchires will be here soon . . . don't be afraid. It looks like a monster, but with one brain shared between fifty heads, it isn't very clever." He told us what Hec would look like and how it had been useful in Troy—scaring the guards away from the walls.

And that's when I had my idea. An idea that COULD work.

★★★

The Hecatonchires landed with a clatter of wings in the center of the tent circle. If the warriors were afraid, then they didn't show it. Theus had told me what to expect, but it was still a weird sight. "Hello, boys!" ten of the heads said.

"Hello, Hec," Theus said and stepped forward. "It's good to see you!"

"Is it?" Head 35 said. Head 7 added, "That's odd. We spent all our life in the underworld. Humans were sent down there, and when they saw us, they screamed!" Head 37 agreed. "That's right. No one's *ever* said that it's good to see me!"

"Well, we are pleased, aren't we?" Theus said and

swung around the circle to include us all.

"Yes!" we all cried.

"But why?" Head 35 asked.

"Because you are a legend. We've heard what you did in Troy—battered the walls till the guards fled," Theus said. "We were just saying, we could use a Hecatonchires if we're going to attack Eden City, weren't we?"

Again we all nodded and agreed.

"That's strange," Head 25 put in, "because we've come here tonight to help you to do exactly the same thing!"

"We know . . ." I began, until Pa slapped a hand around my big mouth and hissed, "No, we're not *supposed* to know that!"

"Mng-Mng!" I said (which, as you know, was supposed to be, "Sor-ry!").

"The moon rises at midnight," Theus said. "We will go into action then." He looked at me. "I don't like the plan. But I don't see any other way."

Pa added, "If *you're* worried about the plan, then how do you think *I* feel?"

★★★

Sheriff Spade sat in the Storm Inn and pulled on his

mustache nervously.[34] The mayor patted his arm, filled his beer mug, and leaned toward him. "Don't worry," he said. "If a wooden horse is the best they can come up with, then we have nothing to fear from the Wild People."

"The people of Eden City are getting hungry," the sheriff said. "Another week, and they'll be getting angry. They'll turn against us. They'll make us hand the Wild People's princess back and stop this siege."

The mayor's little eyes glittered in the candlelight. "If that happens, then we must force the Wild People to go away."

"We haven't got enough bullets and powder," Sheriff Spade groaned. "We could have gone out and killed them all if that Dr. Dee had kept his promise and brought us fresh powder and guns."

"We'll deal with him some other time. We may not have enough powder to attack, but we have enough to defend."

"But if we *don't* attack, we'll just stay here till we starve and the Eden City people rebel, Mayor

---

34   No, I wasn't there myself, but the bar manager was. Later, when I went back to Eden City, I heard his story and put it together. It almost happened the way I tell it—and is *almost* as good as some stories get.

Makepeace. We've *lost* thanks to that showman with the balloon."

"We don't need bullets while we have the princess. I have a second plan. We simply put her in a cradle and hang the cradle over the side of the Eden City walls. The Running Bear brat will hear his little sister crying as she gets hungry."

"He won't give in."

"Then he'll hear her *stop* crying after a while. *That* is the worst sound of all. The silence will be like poison in his ear. He'll think she's dying. He *will* give in. And then . . ."

"And then we take over the plains from here to the mountains," the sheriff said and sipped his beer and smacked his lips.

"You and me, Spade. We will own it," the mayor breathed. "Thousands of acres of rich land. And we will sell it to settlers and farmers for five dollars an acre. Riches beyond your dreams, Spade. Beyond your dreams." The mayor's greed gripped his throat and made his voice hoarse. "That baby will make us rich, rich, *rich, rich, RICH!*"

The sheriff stopped with his beer mug halfway to his mouth. "So shouldn't we be guarding the baby if she's that precious?"

"Waters will take care of it. You'll see. Everything will work out fine."

★★★

Achilles sat on the floor of the Temple of the Hero and sharpened the blade of his spear. Paris sat next to him and worked on his arrowheads.

"Why are we here?" Paris asked.

"Because the Avenger told us that it's a good place to wait," Achilles said for the fifth time. "The Avenger is in the sky over the city waiting for the balloon to arrive. As soon as it starts to come down, he'll call us, and we'll fight off Theus' friends while the Avenger grabs Theus."

"But why are we *here*?" Paris asked.

"I've just told you!" Achilles exploded and shook the cobwebs from the walls.

"I know. I know you said that. But *why* is it a good place to wait? Why are we in a temple and who is the hero?" Paris went on.

Achilles rose and stretched. "No one ever comes here, it seems. And the hero? His statue is over there by the altar."

"It's covered up. I can't see his face," Paris complained.

"That's to keep the dust off."

"Can we take a look?" Paris asked.

"A look?"

"At the statue. See what this Eden City hero looks like?"

"It will probably look like me," Achilles said and walked across the dusty floor to the altar.

It was lit by a candle—the only light in the cold and gloomy temple. Achilles lifted the corner of the cloth and looked underneath it. "Well, well, well . . . would you believe it?"

"That's odd," Paris said with a frown.

"Very odd," Achilles agreed and lowered the cloth again.

★★★

The Avenger hung on its huge wings, high over the plains. It was sure Prometheus, the Fire Thief, was down there somewhere. But he would be lost in the swarms of Wild People. It was best to stick to the plan and wait for the god to enter the city and try to rescue the baby.

The Avenger knew that they would use the balloon. They would light the fire underneath the basket and rise into the air. The Fire Thief would be lifted by the power of the fire that Prometheus gave to the humans. It was fire that would carry Prometheus into the city. It was fire that would carry Prometheus to his destruction. The Avenger liked that idea. "Serves him right," he cawed as he soared.

But the balloon lay where it had landed. The firebox was cold and still. It was close to midnight now, and no one moved to touch the empty bag of the balloon.

The grass of the plains rippled in the thin moonlight, and the Avenger's eagle eyes saw people moving toward the city. A Wild People boy, a girl, and a tall man in a top hat.

If they were planning a rescue, then Theus was not with them. The Avenger swooped down low and saw that the boy was carrying a thin rope and the girl held a leather bag, while the man dragged a wooden tube on wheels behind him.

A little farther behind, the Avenger spotted the Hecatonchires as it lumbered along behind them. It wondered who they were, and it kept watching. The Avenger understood. This little army would attack the walls and drive the defenders back. But Prometheus would not climb the walls here. "Of course he won't!" the Avenger hissed. "The city will rush to defend the west wall. Prometheus will climb the wall somewhere else. Maybe he'll even come in from the east—the river!"

That was a clever plan, the Avenger decided. It had figured it out. The Wild People had lots of canoes on the river. While the defenders hurried to the west wall, Prometheus would slip quietly onto the quayside, steal the baby, and escape.

"I'm a fool!" the big bird howled. "Getting to the baby will be easy. But it would be tricky to climb back over the walls with a child. It would make much more sense to come by the river. I see it all now! And if he does slip past me, I have those fools Achilles and Paris waiting to snatch him at the Temple of the Hero. Prometheus will be mine before sunrise."

The Avenger cackled with a noise that sounded like a strangled rooster.[35] It beat its golden-brown wings and climbed high. Then it half closed those wings and sped down toward the quayside. It landed close to the Storm Inn and walked across the road to

35 I know this because, of course, I was on the plains below when the Avenger cackled. I guess the miserable monster didn't do a lot of laughing, and that's why its laugh sounded so strained.

hide in the dark alley by the side.

A small figure with a dirty handkerchief stepped out and threw an arm around the Avenger's neck. In his hand was a knife with a broken blade. "Your money or your life?" the little robber growled.

"Oh, not you again, Mr. Waters. Go away, will you? I'm busy."

"Oops! Sorry, sir. Didn't recognize you," the old man said. "Guess I'll go and rob someone else."

"Yes, you do that."

"Good night!"

"Oh, I'll have a *very* good night."

But the Avenger was wrong. The Avenger was double wrong.

Wrong about Theus coming from the river.

Wrong about having a good night . . .

SEVENTEEN

EDEN CITY—1795, MIDNIGHT

How would you do it? Climb into an enemy city, rescue a baby, AND get her out of the city? Don't know, do you? Now, here's the thing. Neither did I. Oh, yes, I'll tell you how I planned to do those things. But Pa, Running Bear, and Prometheus were so dazzled by my plan that they missed the one thing WRONG with it. There would be no escape for ME at the end of it. No plan is perfect—not even mine. But I didn't know that then.

The Hecatonchires lumbered along and stopped around 100 paces from the wooden walls of Eden City. It began to pick up stones from the windy plains. I was hoping to surprise the defenders, but, with Hec, there was no chance. He just *had* to talk to himself . . .

"Left . . . two-three-four-five . . . and right . . . two-three-four-five!" the heads chanted. "Left . . . two-three-four-five . . . and right . . . two-three-four-oops! Well, it's a bit dark out here!" After a minute 100 rocks were clutched in 100 hands. "Righty-ho! Ready when you are."

There was excited chatter from the guards on the walls of Eden City as they stared into the moonlit gloom. They saw the 50-headed monster, but they didn't quite believe it. They were slow to raise their muskets.

Too slow.

Suddenly, 100 arms threw 100 rocks at them. Some clattered off the wooden walls—thunk—some sailed over into the streets behind them—clatter— and some bounced off the heads of the slower soldiers—ouch.

It went silent. In the dim light the guards shrank down behind the parapet and heard distant voices . . . "Left . . . two-three-four-five . . . and right . . . two-three-four-five!"

Guard Hank Plank of River Row muttered, "Got to go home. I just remembered . . . I need to put the cat out."

"Is it on fire?" his friend Joe Scrimger asked.

Hank shuffled over to the ladder and jumped down two rungs at a time. "I think he's scared," Joe scoffed. "It'll take more than a hundred stones to scare me . . ."

"Righty-ho! Ready when you are," came the cheerful voice from the plains. There was a thunderous rumble as rocks rained down.

"Oh! It would take more than a hundred rocks . . . but two hundred are just ninety-nine too many. No one will miss me if I go home to put my wife out!" Joe Scrimger whined and headed for the ladder. It was tough getting down—tough when 20 other guards were all trying to climb down the same ladder.

"We don't get paid for this," a voice grumbled in the darkness. "Careful, you're standing on my fingers!"

"No . . . it's someone else's turn to do guard duty," another voice agreed.

By the time the third storm of stones sailed over the walls, they were deserted. The gallant guards of Eden City had torn back through the twisted streets of their city and were hiding under their blankets. Fifty cats had been put out . . . even though not one of them was on fire.

Only an old man wandered through the deepest shadows of the darkest alleys with a dirty handkerchief around his face, looking for someone to rob.

Outside the walls we sensed the silence of the city. The soft sighing of the wind through the grass was answered by the yowls of 50 sleepy cats. "Time to go," I said.

Theus looked unhappy. "This is a job for me," he said for the 20th time.

For the 20th time, I told him, "No. You've done your part. You've figured out where they're hiding the baby princess."

"I could be wrong," he argued.

"That's a chance I'll have to take," I said, and I closed my eyes and tried to remember the map that he had drawn me.

Running Bear fastened the light rope around the end of an arrow and fired it at the wall. It struck the parapet and sank into the wood quite deeply . . . at least I was hoping it was deep.

He took the loose end of the rope and tied it around the heaviest thing he could find . . . a leg of the Hecatonchires.

"Step back, Hec," Pa ordered. The monster

obeyed. The rope was tight. Pa checked it. "Perfect," he told me. "As long as the creature doesn't move."

"I'm not a creature," Hec complained. "I'm a people just like you."

"Except you have fifty heads," Pa told him.

"Yeah, and fifty times as many hurt feelings!"

"Sorry, sorry, Hec," I said quickly. "I am *so* grateful to you. I wish there was some way I could repay you."

"Huh! Huh!" the monster said and giggled. "You could give me a kiss before you go."

"Oh, all right," I agreed. Hec lifted me up with his lower hands and passed me up, hand over hand, till I reached his shoulders. Then I kissed him . . . 50 times.

"Wow, I've never been kissed before," he said with a sigh.

"Look, can we just get on with this rescue?" Pa snapped.

"We're ready," Running Bear said.

I stepped onto the rope and began to walk along it, climbing all the time. The wind from the plains rocked me, but I knew that I would never fall. It was just too important. Even the cats had fallen silent by the time I reached the top of the wall and climbed over and onto the parapet. The guards had all left, I was pleased to see.

I tugged on the rope. I felt it go slack as Hec stepped forward. Pa untied it from his leg and tied it to the cannon. I hauled the cannon carefully up the wall. Even though it was made out of wood, it took all of my strength. Sweat ran down my face and made the palms of my hands slippery. I didn't want the cannon to tip and spill what was in the barrel.

It was hard to heave it over the wall, and I was sweating. Then I lowered it down the other side and into the street below. Now there was no way back for me. I had to continue with the plan.

I climbed carefully down the ladder. There was no hurry. I had all night.

I reached inside the barrel of the cannon and pulled out the two bundles. I unwrapped the soft one—a bunch of clothes, a hat, boots, a wig, and my Gregory the Great mustache.

I dressed carefully. I may not be able to shape-shift like Zeus, but I could do a good job of looking like someone else.

The second bundle was a leather bag. I slipped that

inside my jacket pocket.

Finally I gathered stones from the street—stones that Hec had thrown—and put them under the barrel of the cannon so that it pointed up to the dark sky. I set the cannon so that it would fire at a touch of the trigger.

I closed my eyes and tried to picture Theus' map. I knew it would be too dark to read a map in the dingy Eden City streets, and I didn't dare show a light.

It was a slow and stumbling journey. For some reason there were a lot of cats wandering around, green eyes glowing angrily, meowing at doors.

An old man stepped out from one dark alley and waved a broken knife in front of me. "Your money or your life?" he croaked. "I am the Phantom of the Night!"

The rescue plan was that I'd dress and act like Sheriff Spade. I had to put the plan into action a little earlier than I wanted to. "Put that knife down, or I'll arrest you in the name of the law!" I said in the sheriff's creaky voice.

"Is that you, Sheriff?"

"It is."

"Oh, this just hasn't been my night."

A little starlight drifted down into the street, but my eyes were used to the dark now. "Say . . . didn't I buy you a drink at the Storm Inn last night?" I asked angrily. I'd felt sorry for this old man, and now he was trying to rob me.

"No, Sheriff, *I* bought *you* a drink!"

"Ah, yes . . . oh . . . ah, so you did, old man. But wasn't there a girl in the bar who bought you a drink? That sweet and pretty girl that was with Dr. Dee's Carnival of Danger?"

"I wouldn't call her pretty, but, yes, she did buy me a drink," the old man admitted.

"So you should be ashamed of yourself!" I told him.

"Why?"

"Because someone shows you kindness, and that's how you repay them," I raged.

"But she was a sucker. I always take money from suckers—same as you, Sheriff Spade."

"Ah, yes . . . oh . . . ah, well, it's time you changed your ways."

"And will you be changing *your* ways, Sheriff?" he asked me. "I get a few cents from people . . . but you're planning to rob the Wild People of tens of thousands of dollars worth of land."

"That's different," I told him. "Now take me to Mrs. Waters' baby farm." If anyone could guide me through these dark and twisting streets, it would be this old robber.

"I will . . . I was just on my way there now."

"You were? Why?"

"Because I live there—you know that, Sheriff. I'm Josh Waters, and my wife runs the baby farm!"

"I knew that," I said quickly. "I was just . . . checking that you are who you say you are."

"Say, are you all right, Sheriff?"

"Perfectly. Now lead on," I said and grabbed his greasy belt at the back so that I didn't lose him in the dark.

We trotted on through mud and cats till we came to the dusty window and looked into a room lit by a single candle. "Now, here's the plan," I told Josh Waters . . . even though I'd just made up a new plan. "We are going to send the Wild People's baby back to them. They'll go away, and we'll take over the land. You are going to help me."

"Why am I going to do that, Sheriff?" he asked.

I reached inside my jacket and pulled out Pa's money. "For fifty dollars," I said.

"A hundred," he said.

I thought about it. The well-fed baby was Princess Prairie Rose. The others were just poor kids whose parents didn't want them. They were skinny and weak. I changed my plan again. "I'll pay a hundred . . . *IF* you help me send *ALL* the babies over to the Wild People . . . They'll care for them better than your wife."

The old man cackled, and his breath was more sour than the Eden City gutter that we stood in. "Heh! Heh! For a hundred dollars, I'll throw in my wife!"

"There are six babies in there that I can see. We can carry three each . . . you go in and get them."

"Why me?"

"Because I am paying you a hundred dollars and because if your wife wakes up and catches you, then you can think up some story."[36]

The old man unlocked the door, and a moment later he appeared with three sleepy babies in his arms. "Fifty dollars worth here," he said.

---

36 In my first plan I was just going to break open the door. If Mrs. Waters had caught me, I was going to use the money to buy the princess off her. Old Josh saved me a lot of trouble—even if it cost me half the money that Pa had taken from the Eden City people. Well, it wasn't our money anyway.

I paid him. He slipped back in and came out with Prairie Rose and another two babies. I knew it was the princess because she was chubbier and better fed than the other children, who were as thin as rainwater. She was sleeping soundly. "Another fifty," he said.

I paid him again.

The babies were too weak to cry, so no one disturbed us as we hurried back to the walls.

"Hey! I'll use that hundred dollars to buy a new knife," the old man said with a chuckle. "Some feller in a feathered cloak smashed my old one."

"Feathered cloak?"

"Yep! And a mouth like a beak."

"The Avenger," I said and shivered. I remembered what Theus had told me about it. "Where is it now?"

"I left it on the kitchen table."

"The Avenger's on your kitchen table?"

"No, the broken knife!"

"I mean where is the feller with the feathered cloak?"

"Hiding in an alley at the side of the Storm Inn," he told me.

That piece of news was going to be worth the

hundred dollars that I had paid him.

"Where are we going?" the old man asked.

"Wait and see," I said as I reached the spot where I'd hidden the cannon. I took off my black coat and laid my three babies on top of it while I ran up the steps to the top of the wall. I looked out over the windy plains and saw big Hec sitting on the ground plucking stalks of grass to chew in each of his mouths. "Hec!" I hissed. "There'll be *six* of them!"

"Not a problem for me, Nell . . . I can manage a hundred!"

"Don't drop any," I warned and ran back down.

I took Prairie Rose from old Josh and slipped her into the barrel of the cannon. I checked it carefully, took aim, and fired. The bundle wrapped in the dirty gray blanket shot up into the dead air of Eden City, over the walls, and into the clean, free air of the plains.

Then I followed with the other five sleeping children.

I raced up the steps to the top of the walls and looked out. Hec waved his 94 free arms. "They're safe," he cried and turned to walk back to the Wild People's camp.

I pulled up the rope that I'd used to lower the cannon. I threw it out onto the plains.

"Hey! Who's going to hold the rope?"

The rope hung down the wall. I guessed that I would have to climb down that rope rather than walk across it like a tightrope.

But I couldn't climb down the rope—because someone was climbing up it . . .

EIGHTEEN

EDEN CITY—THE STORM INN, THE WEST WALL,
THE TEMPLE OF THE HERO (AND OTHER PLACES)

*There were so many things about to happen that it's hard
to get them in the right order so that you understand. It
is tough being a writer. Maybe I should try something
simpler—like climbing mountains blindfolded.*

The Avenger waited in the alley by the side of the
Storm Inn. Even in the darkness, it could see that
the Wild People's canoes were being paddled *away*
from the city. "They'll land and launch another
attack on another part of the walls. A single canoe
will slip in for the rescue. Oh, it's a cunning plan.
There'll be no one left to guard the waterfront."

The Avenger didn't notice that there was already

no one guarding the waterfront.

★★★

Inside the Storm Inn the mayor and Sheriff Spade drank their ale and chatted about how they would spend their fortunes. "I'll build myself a house in the foothills, away from this stinking city. I may buy myself one of those balloons to fly around the mountains!" the sheriff said.

"The Wild People will be in the mountains," the mayor reminded him.

The sheriff frowned. "Speaking of the Wild People, we should be guarding the waterfront in case they decide to land and rescue the baby."

"Another drink, and then we'll go," the mayor said.

The innkeeper had gone to bed hours ago and left the two men with a barrel of ale to serve themselves. As guards go, they were as much use to Eden City as a comb to a bald man.

★★★

I stood at the top of the west wall of Eden City and shivered. Who was climbing up the rope? I stepped back and was ready to make a run for it.

A man's head appeared. He had long hair and a handsome face. "Theus!" I squawked. "You're not supposed to be here. The Avenger's in the city.

We agreed that I'd do the rescue alone."

He placed an arm around my shoulder and hugged me. "I know, and you did it brilliantly."

In the starlit darkness he couldn't see me blush, but I felt my face burning. "So why are you here?"

"I came to look in the Temple of the Hero. I have to find a true human hero so that Zeus can set me free. Then I have to go to the Storm Inn to get my wings and fly home."

"You can't go to the Storm Inn," I said, and I told him what old Mr. Waters had said.

"Then I'm trapped in Eden City," he said softly.

"No," I said. "*You* go to the temple—I'll get your wings from the Storm Inn and bring them to you!"

Theus looked at me curiously. "I think I've found a human hero in you," he said softly.

Now my face turned so red that I was surprised it didn't light the city streets like a red moon. I turned to walk down the steps into the city.

"No, Theus, I'm just having fun. This beats tightrope walking for excitement." I laughed. "I'm no hero."[37]

---

37 Go on and argue if you like. Call me a hero—or heroine—if you want. I am much too modest to ever admit it. I only did what any brave, unselfish, wonderful, and beautiful girl would do.

He hugged me again. "I'll see you at the Temple of the Hero at sunrise," he said. There was a faint line of charcoal gray on the black horizon over the river. I guessed that sunrise wasn't all that far away.

"Let me go first," I said. "We don't want the old man to see you."

He nodded and stayed in the shadow of the wall. I found Mr. Waters sitting on the cannon. "Take me to the Storm Inn," I told him. "I need to collect something. Then I need you to guide me to the Temple of the Hero."

"*Guide* you, Sheriff? You've lived in Eden City all your life.[38] Why would you want me to guide you?"

"For twenty dollars," I said.

"Fifty."

"Ten's my final offer," I said.

"It's a deal," he cackled, and I handed over a single dollar. In the darkness he couldn't tell the difference. It was nice to make a sucker of him for a change.

He hobbled through the streets, and I held onto

---

38 Yes, I'd forgotten that I was playing the part of the sheriff. I played so many roles in the carnival that I often forgot who I was supposed to be. I had to look at my costume to remind myself. I'll never forget the day that Miss Cobweb dived into the flaming pool instead of Captain Dare.

his belt. Only the guards who had run away were awake. They were waiting for the Wild People to rampage through the streets, break into their homes, and scalp them in their beds.

Some guards hid under the covers, some hid under the beds, and some just crossed their fingers. When morning came and they discovered that the Wild People had gone away, they swore that their finger crossing had worked.

We arrived at the Storm Inn in a half light. I sensed the feathered evil in the alley and crept past.

"Stay here, Mr. Waters. I may need you to guide me to the Temple of the Hero." He opened his mouth to speak, but I put in, "And, yes, I'll pay you."

I reached for the handle of the tavern door, and it turned in my hand.

I jumped back as if it had been a living snake. But it was only the mayor, turning it on the inside as he stepped out. He looked at me and blinked. He looked over his shoulder at the sheriff who stood behind him. "I think I had too much beer," the mayor murmured as he rubbed his eyes. "I'm seeing two sheriffs!"

"No, you're not," I said. "That man is a fake and a phony! He's here to steal the Wild People's princess.

I arrest him in the name of the law!"

The sheriff staggered out into the roadway, pushed past the mayor, and peered at me. "It's a mirror!"

I had to act quickly—or the arrested one would be me and Theus would be trapped. "In fact, I don't arrest you . . . I . . . er . . . send you back to the Wild People in their boats."

"You what?"

"Mayor! Mr. Waters! Grab that phony sheriff and . . . and throw him in the river!" I ordered. "Let him swim to the Wild People's canoes where he came from."

The two men hurried to obey me. That's what fear and panic do to people. All they needed was someone to give them an order, and they were happy to obey.

Sheriff Spade struggled and spluttered. The men slithered over the greasy cobbles to the river. When they reached the edge, the sheriff found a new strength to struggle. "I'm too old to die!" he cried and grabbed at the mayor as he toppled in. The two fell in the filthy water together and clung onto some ropes that hung from a ship. "It's cold!" the mayor wailed.

I didn't have time to listen to them. I ran into the inn and lifted a trapdoor in the stage. The wings were there just as Theus had told me they would be.

They were lighter than a spider's web. I tucked them under my arm and ran outside. The sky was pearl gray now, and I felt as if a thousand candles were showing the Avenger what I was up to.

The Phantom of the Night had shuffled across the quayside to help the men in the water. "Hurry, Mr. Waters!" I called to the old man who was helping the mayor up to the quayside. "Get back here!"

"In a minute, Sheriff," he said as he heaved and struggled with the heavy, soaked men. He was made heavier by the wet sheriff clinging onto his coattails.

"We don't have a minute," I moaned. With my free hand, I pulled out all the cash that was left. "Look, this is all yours if you get me to the Temple of the Hero before sunrise."

Mr. Waters grinned his toothless grin. He let the mayor go, and I saw him fall back into the water. Mr. Waters hobbled across to me. "Why didn't you say so?"

I followed him and half pushed him through the streets. But I knew I'd made a mistake—a mistake as big as Pa had made when he forgot to check the wind. (Of course you've spotted it because you are so clever.) Inside the Temple of the Hero, Paris turned his head sharply. "Someone's coming! Footsteps in the courtyard outside," he whispered to Achilles, who was resting against the altar. "It's probably Theus."

"Ooh! What do we do?" Achilles asked, and his voice quivered.

"Hold him till the Avenger gets here. That's what it told us to do."

"We can't hold a god!" Achilles groaned. "You're a human. And I'm only a half god. He'll destroy us. I'm leaving."

Paris jumped to his feet and grabbed at Achilles' tunic. "You can't. There's only one door, and Theus is coming through it now!"

"Oh!" Achilles gasped. He jumped onto the altar. A cloth covered the statue. He lifted the cloth and jumped underneath it just as the door creaked open and he heard Theus say, "Paris! What are you doing here?"

"Er . . . good morning, Theus—just waiting for the Avenger. He told us to wait here for him."

"Us?"

"Ah . . . yes . . . Achilles was with me. He's just gone to get him."

Theus marched across the dusty temple floor and pushed Paris aside. "Then I'll have to be quick." He lifted the sheet that covered the statue. Carved on the base were the words, "The hero— he saved us."

Then he lifted the cloth higher. The figure underneath was frozen in fear. Theus breathed, "What a wonderful statue. It's almost as if it was alive."

"Yes," Paris said and laughed nervously.

Theus stepped back and let the cloth fall back in place. "But it's a statue of Achilles. After all my searching, Achilles is the hero of Eden City."

"Well, he was a hero in Troy too," Paris said. "Not as good as me, of course. I killed him. But Achilles was a hero of sorts."

"Hang on. Achilles is a half god. I need to find a *human* hero for Zeus. This is no use to me," Theus moaned. "Now I'll have to fly for my life. I hope that Helen gets here in time."

"Helen of Troy?" Paris asked. "The face that launched two hundred ships?"

"No . . . another, better Helen," Theus said and strode to the door. He looked out into the courtyard. A beautiful young girl was running past an old man.[39] She was carrying his wings under her arm. Remember, I told you that I'd made a mistake? And, of course, you spotted it.

I hadn't just told Mr. Waters where I was headed with the wings. The Avenger with his eagle ears would have heard me too.

When I reached the mouth of the alleyway that led to the Temple of the Hero, I glanced over my shoulder. The shuffling shape of a hunched and feathered figure was following.

I pushed past Mr. Waters and raced down the alleyway. Theus was stepping out of the temple, followed by Paris.

"Sorry, Theus, the Avenger followed me," I panted. "Hurry, or it'll catch you!"

Theus strapped on the wings and looked toward the alley. "Too late," a voice said. The Avenger shuffled past the old man and stopped. Its glittering eyes were as deep as a bottomless well. If beaks could grin, then its hooked bill was smiling like a cat with a trapped rat.

"Go!" I groaned.

---

39 Yes, even under the disguise of a sheriff, he could tell that she was beautiful. Who was this gallant girl? Oh, come on, who do you think?

Theus shook his head. "He'll only follow," he said and sighed. "Thanks for trying, Helen of Eden." He held me by the shoulders. "But I failed to find the human hero. I'm finished."

I felt a scalding wetness on my cheeks and realized that I was crying.

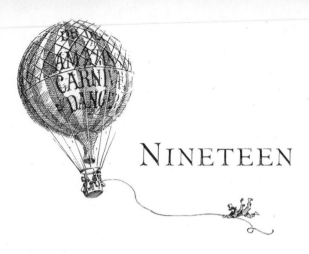

NINETEEN

EDEN CITY—THE TEMPLE OF THE HERO

Well? What did you expect? A happy ending? I'm telling you my true story here. In real life, things don't always end happily. So good, kind Theus was caught and doomed. Weep along with me. And then remember . . . in real life, things don't always end happily. Not always. But sometimes they do . . .

Helen of Eden doesn't give up without a fight.

The Avenger walked slowly forward to the three steps that led up to the temple where Theus stood.

I snatched Paris' sword from his belt, ran across the courtyard, and handed it to the old man. "This feathered feller has a thousand dollars tucked under his wing. Rob him, and it's all yours!"

216

"You want me to do a robbery, Sheriff?"

I tore off the mustache and the hat. "I'm not the sheriff."

"Then who did I throw in the river?"

"The real sheriff," I said. "Now, quickly, get the money!"

The old man trotted after the Avenger and jumped on its back. He held the sword to its throat—he was careful to keep it out of the way of the crunching beak this time.

The Avenger wasn't expecting this, and it toppled over onto its back. "Fly, Theus! Fly!" I cried.

The great god jumped into the air and circled over the temple. "Good-bye, my Helen . . . you're worth *ten* thousand ships!"

In moments, he had disappeared into the clouds. Achilles came out onto the steps and glanced at the struggling pair on the ground. Paris looked at him. "Theus thought that *you* were the hero," Paris said. "He never saw the statue of the real hero."

"No," Achilles mumbled, ashamed.

"It was a rotten thing to do to him," Paris said. "We owe him something in return." Achilles nodded. As the Avenger finally threw off the old man, the two Greek warriors threw themselves onto the eagle-bodied monster and wrestled him back down to the ground. The Avenger clawed and slashed with his beak, but the two men finally acted like the heroes that they were supposed to be.

At last they knelt, one on each of the Avenger's wings, and the bird screamed its hatred. "You will go to Hades for this," it cried.

"You were going to take us to Hades anyway, weren't you? Once we helped you capture Theus, you'd have betrayed us, wouldn't you?"

"Of course," the Avenger croaked. "Of course."

It lay, helpless, on its back and stared up at the sky. Then its eyes were fixed on something up there. I wondered if Theus had been foolish enough to return. I looked up. A red-and-white striped balloon drifted over the top of the temple, and Pa waved down from the basket.

"The wind has changed, Nell!" he shouted. "We're going back to East River City! We'll be free with all that money!"

Then he threw down a rope, which I gripped with both hands. I didn't tell him that the money was all gone—he may have dropped me! I'd tell him that later.

Pa hauled me up into the basket and turned to put more straw on the fire. The balloon leaped into the clouds and carried me away from the filthy city and into the clean clouds that glowed gold in the rising sun.

A creature with 50 heads and 100 arms flew past us on its way to the stars. "Good-bye, Hec!" I called, and he waved every arm. Head 35 said, "I'm on my way to a planet I saw on my way here . . . the people there are normal. They ALL have fifty heads! And the girls are gorgeous!" And he was gone.

Pa looked up at the monster and said, "One day we'll all be able to fly like that. Go where we want in the air, not be blown by the wind."

"No, we won't!" I mocked. "Anyway, it's more fun going where the wind blows you. It's more of an adventure. If humans were supposed to fly, the gods would have given us wings."

Pa jammed his top hat firmly on his head as the wind caught the balloon and sent us speeding toward the sunrise side of the river. "One day we'll fly, I tell you. I know it. Trust me—I'm a doctor."

I looked at him and laughed. "No, you're not, Pa. No, you're not!"

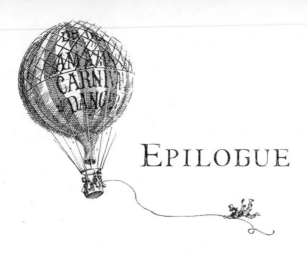

EPILOGUE

EDEN CITY—1857

That's the end of my story—the story of what happened to me back in 1795. What happened to Helen of Eden City since then? That would take a dozen books to tell. But let me tell you the parts that matter for this story . . . [40]

Twenty years passed before I returned to Eden City. By then, the people had forgotten the showman and the girl who had tricked them out of their money.

I went there on a visit. And now, 62 years later, I'm back.

---

40 How Achilles and Paris ended up is in the books of legends. There you'll see that they went to the Isles of the Blessed . . . maybe Zeus felt sorry for them. Or maybe not. For Achilles . . . yes, Achilles . . . ended up with his old enemy Helen of Troy. The face that launched 100 ships. Life is strange. Legend is even stranger.

The city has changed. It is dirtier and more twisted than ever, with factories spewing purple smoke over the place like a vast umbrella.

The Wild People are gone, and so are the city's wooden walls. The settlers have moved on to the plains. They used their guns to drive Running Bear and his people into the mountains, where only a few remain now.

Theus would have blamed himself. But, knowing human greed the way I do, I think nothing could have stopped the evil Eden City people from reaching out and taking what they wanted.

So why do I want to stay in this cruel and crumbling city?

I remembered that Theus will be coming to the city for his first visit in 1858. I've decided that I'd like to see him one more time. Though he won't know me . . . he won't have met me. And, anyway, I'm an old woman now, not the young girl who helped him free a princess.

But I did go to the Temple of the Hero one day. I wanted to see just who this hero was.

The temple was decayed and dusty. A faded sign said, "Caretaker wanted. Apply to Mayor Mucklethrift."

I walked in.

The statue stood underneath its tattered cloth. I pulled the cloth off the carved stone figure and looked at the face.

I was shocked. And puzzled. And pleased. And sad.

I covered it up again and went to the city hall.

I got myself the job of caretaker. I care—a lot.

Theus will return within the year.

I hope that I live long enough to see him. I know that he won't find the end of his quest there because in his time he's already been to 1858 and failed.

The answer lies somewhere in the past. People like me can't go back.

But I pray, by whatever gods there may be, that Theus finds what he's looking for.

I know he will. I'm sure he will.

GLOSSARY

Achilles: A strong and fearless warrior in the Greek war against the Trojans. As an infant, his mother dipped him into the River Styx, which made him invulnerable everywhere but the heel by which she held him.

The Avenger/The Fury: An eagle with god-given powers, he was commanded by Zeus to rip out Prometheus' liver every day.

The Hecatonchires: A giant Greek monster with incredible strength and ferocity. It had 100 arms and 50 heads.

Helen: The queen of Sparta. She was so beautiful that men would start wars to be with her. When she was kidnapped by Paris, this started the Trojan War.

Hera: The queen of the Olympian deities. She was a daughter of Cronus and Rhea and the wife and sister of Zeus. Hera was mostly worshipped as a goddess of marriage and birth.

Hermes: The son of Zeus and the messenger of the gods. It was his duty to guide the souls of the dead down to the underworld.

Paris: The son of King Priam of Troy. He kidnapped Helen, the queen of Sparta, which started the Trojan War.

Polyxena: A beautiful Trojan princess, she was the youngest daughter of King Priam.

Prometheus: A Titan who stole fire from Zeus and the gods. In punishment, Zeus commanded that Prometheus be chained for eternity to the Caucasus Mountains. There, an eagle would eat his liver, and each day the liver would regrow again, making the punishment endless.

Troy: A legendary city during the period of ancient Greece. The scene of the Trojan War, which lasted for many years.

Zeus: The youngest son of Cronus and Rhea, he was the supreme ruler of Mount Olympus and of the pantheon of gods who resided there. He upheld the law, justice, and morals and was the spiritual leader of both gods and humans.

HERE IS A SPECIAL PREVIEW OF THE FIRST
CHAPTER FROM *THE FIRE THIEF FIGHTS BACK*,
THE THIRD AND FINAL PART OF THE GRIPPING
FIRE THIEF TRILOGY!

ANCIENT GREECE—BUT I'M NOT SURE WHEN

The first part of my tale is from a book of legends. "Ha!"
you say. "Legends are just old lies. I want to know the
TRUTH." Well, I have met one of the legends, and I
know that HIS story is true. So why shouldn't the other
legends be true? Anyway, it's the only way we can explain
what happened to me when I was a boy. And THAT was
true, because I was there at the time. SO let's start with
ancient Greece, and stop interrupting me with your
moaning about the "truth," will you?

"What do you want, fat face?" the young god asked.
He wore a helmet with wings and had wings on his
heels. He carried a rod with a snake wrapped around
it. Even the snake looked shocked.

"You can't sss-speak to your mother like that,
Hermes!"

"Oh, go shed your skin, you rattail of a reptile,"

i

Hermes replied and polished his nails on his white tunic.

"You'll be sss-sorry you sss-said that," the sss-snake his-sss-sed.

A goddess lay on a golden couch and scowled at the winged god. She was so beautiful that you could hardly bear to look at her. Her dark hair fell in a swirling cloud over her shoulders, yet she never used curlers and hardly ever had to dye it.

If you *could* bear to look at her, you'd have seen her face turn red with rage, and her lips pulled back tightly over her gleaming teeth. (And she never had to go to a dentist.) Somehow she controlled her temper.

"I am Hera, queen of the gods, wife to the mighty Zeus, and ruler of the world. Speak to me like that, and I will punish you like no god has ever been punished, Hermes."

He blew on his nails and gave a warm smile. "Oh, knock it off, Mom. You won't punish your dear little Hermes."

"Why not?" she spat.

"Because you *need* me! I am the messenger of the gods. If you didn't have *me* to run errands, you'd be tramping from here to the Caucasus, from Troy to

Atlantis, just to make mischief."

She narrowed her eyes. "Mischief?"

"Yes. You *know* you like to go around making trouble, because you get *bored*, don't you, Mom?"

She raised her beautiful chin and looked through the window of the marble palace to the lake below and the mountains beyond. "Mischief is my job. It's what gods do."

Hermes walked across the shining marble floor, his winged sandals fluttering. He leaned over the goddess. "Anyway, you must *want* something, or you wouldn't have called for me."

"Maybe."

"Oh, come on. What is it? You want me to kidnap some human maiden that's caught Zeus' eye? It wouldn't be the first time. Or turn a girl into a swan just for spite?"

Hera glared at him, and then her face became softer and almost tearful. Her voice was low. "It's more serious than that, Hermes. Zeus has gone."

The winged god threw back his head and laughed. "Gone? So? He's always off somewhere, the old goat. He'll be back. He always comes back to Olympus."

Hera blinked away a tear. "Not this time, Hermes.

Not this time."

She looked around to make sure that there were no servants watching and reached under the couch. She pulled out a scroll of yellow parchment and unrolled it carefully. Hermes peered at it. There was a message there but not in the usual stylus and ink.

"What's this?" Hermes asked. Even the snake stretched its neck to look.

Hera explained. "Someone has taken a book, cut out the letters, and stuck them onto the parchment."

"They've ruined the book!" Hermes said and sighed.

Hera shook her head. "What has that got to do with anything, idiot boy? The point is that they sent this message."

"But why didn't they just write it?" Hermes asked.

"Because they didn't want us to know who sent it!" Hera said wisely.

Hermes nodded and read the message:

"Dear Hera,
I have captured Zeus. I cut out the tendons in his wrists and knees. He cannot run. He cannot throw his thunderbolts. He is helpless. He is a prisoner in

Delphyne's cave. I will not tell you where he is unless you bring me his crown so that I can rule the world. You have until sunset to obey, or Zeus will lose an eye, an arm, or a leg every day till, on the last day, he loses his head. I mean it. The crown or your hubby gets it . . . and I don't mean a vacation in Crete.

The secret kidnapper—the Typhon"

Hermes turned as pale as his feathers. "The Typhon? The most hideous creature in the whole world! And now he's going to rule the world."

"Not if you set Zeus free," Hera said softly.

"Not if I set Zeus free," Hermes agreed. Then he swallowed hard. "*ME!*" he squawked. "This is a job for a *hero*—Hercules or Prometheus. Someone who doesn't mind being blasted by a hundred dragon breaths. I'm a messenger, Mom! Why should *I* go? Why can't someone *else* rescue Zeus?"

Hera grabbed her son by the front of his tunic. "Keep your voice down. Listen. Everybody hates Zeus . . ."

"Well, I wouldn't say *everybody*, Mom. I know *you* do . . ."

"If Hades in the underworld hears about this, he'll

be up here like one of your father's thunderbolts. He's always wanted to rule Earth. And Poseidon down in the sea would leap like a dolphin at the chance. We've already had to defeat the revolt of the Alead giants . . ."

"Ugly brutes," Hermes agreed. "Their mother, Gaia, was furious!"

Hera nodded her head quickly. "And that's why Gaia created the Typhon—for revenge." She shook the letter under Hermes' nose. "This is it."

"But you still aren't saying why *I* have to go after the Typhon, Mom. He's a monster."

"He's half human." Hera shrugged.

"Oh, yes!" Hermes squawked. "It's not the human half that I'm worried about! It's the half that has a hundred fire-breathing dragon heads under his arms and the serpents that are wrapped around his legs!"

"Nothing wrong with sss-serpents," Hermes' snake hissed.

"There is when they can stretch out as high as his πhead—and he's as tall as this palace!" Hermes moaned.

"Sss-sorry, I'm sss-sure!"

"Every one of those dragon heads spits fire," Hera

explained. "He can heat rocks with his breath and throw them at you."

The snake sss-sighed. "I can't do that."

Hera turned to Hermes. "You are the only one I can trust. If Poseidon or Hades takes over Olympus, they'll destroy you."

"*Me*? What have *I* ever done? I'm only a poor little messenger of the gods. I never did anyone any harm. Not one single god," Hermes whimpered.

"You are the son of Zeus, and that is enough," Hera explained. "They will crush you—or shut you down in Hades' underworld forever.

Hermes shuddered. "But how can a little old feathered fool like me beat a serpent-snapping, fire-frizzling fiend like the Typhon?"

Hera lay back and thought. "First you have to find your father . . ."

"But the Typhon says in the letter that he won't tell where Zeus is hidden."

"The letter also says that Zeus is a prisoner in Delphyne's cave. The Typhon isn't very bright."

Hermes looked miserable. "Are there no heroes brave enough to fight the Typhon? Someone who could battle with the monster while I sneak into the cave?"

Hera shook her head. "When the Typhon first appeared, the heroes all fled to Egypt or disguised themselves as animals."

"Chickens," Hermes mumbled.

"Yes, chickens—or rabbits or ducks," Hera agreed. "Only Prometheus would have been brave enough to tackle the Typhon."

"Even Prometheus is hiding," Hermes said with a sigh.

"Ah, but he's not hiding from the Typhon," Hera said. "He stole fire from the gods and gave it to the humans. He is being hunted by the eagle-winged Avenger."

"Can't we bring him back? Offer to pardon him if he rescues Zeus?"

Hera shook her head. "He's traveled through time—he's thousands of years into the future. If the Avenger can't find him, then we have no chance. Only Zeus could track down Prometheus . . . and Zeus is a prisoner of the Typhon. It's your job. You're Zeus' son."

Hermes puffed out his cheeks and blew. "And a son's got to do what a son's got to do. I'll go and get my book of maps," he said and fluttered sadly out of the great marble room.

★★★

The god Prometheus was also flying. Flying far out in the galaxy of stars. A strange monster flew by his side. A monster with 50 heads on top of its square body and 100 arms—50 down each side. It was the guardian of the gates of the underworld—the Hecatonchires—and it was escaping.

The two legends slowed as they reached an amber sun and headed for a planet of blue grasslands and green seas.

"Here we are, Hec," Prometheus said as they swooped down toward a village on the planet. "Your home planet."

Head 35 sniffed away a tear. "Home," he said. "The prettiest word ever invented."

"Except for the word 'prettiest,'" Head 57 argued.

Head 35 ignored him. "A planet where everyone has fifty heads and one hundred arms."

They hovered in the clouds. "I'm sure that you'll be very happy here," Prometheus said.

"Oh, I will," Head 35 said. "You could join me, Theus. The Avenger would never find you here."

"I'd feel a little bit out of place," the hero god said and sighed. "I'd be treated like a monster."

"Well, I suppose you are—only one head and two arms. You *are* a little freaky."

"Thanks," Prometheus muttered.

Big Hec nodded all 50 heads. "But I know what you mean. I was like that on Earth. People treated me like some weird alien! Me! I reckon that *they* are the weird ones!"

"I can't imagine why."

"Because I have a hundred arms!" the Hecatonchires cried. "I mean, even your spiders have eight arms, and as for your millipedes . . ."

"Yes, Hec. I'm glad you've found a planet full of your own kind," Theus said and looked down sadly.

"You'll find a home somewhere, Theus," Head 49 said. "But I have a feeling that it will be back on Earth. All you have to do is find a human hero and Zeus will set you free."

"I know," Theus said and nodded his single head. "I've been to the place that they call Eden City. I've visited it twice now. I'm sure that the answer lies down there. I went there in 1858 and again in 1795. Maybe if I go back just a little farther . . . just ten years."

"That's 1785!" the Hecatonchires told him.

"Then 1785 it is," Theus said and slapped the 100-armed monster on the back. "Good-bye, my friend. I hope you find happiness . . . but forgive me if I don't shake hands with you." He laughed. "It would take too long!"

As the Hecatonchires let itself drift down to the green-and-blue planet, it waved 100 hands in farewell.

Theus soared back to the edge of the universe and turned left at the farthest star. That way, he would arrive back on Earth ten years before he left it in 1795.

He sped past meteors and comets through the emptiness toward a little planet that wasn't green and blue like the Hecatonchires' home. It was blue and green. "Home," he cried. "A pretty word."

But as he raced down toward the sunset side of Earth, the god found that there is a lovelier word than "home."

It's the word "hope."